Look what people are saying about Jennifer LaBrecque...

"Jennifer LaBrecque's skill at mixing humor and sensuality is evident in *Really Hot!*, perhaps her finest book yet."
—*Romantic Times BOOKreviews*

"Romance at its best."
—*CataRomance.com* on *Highland Fling*

"Jennifer LaBrecque turns up the heat."
—*Romantic Times BOOKreviews* on *Better Than Chocolate...*

"A vividly emotional and erotic tale about two wonderfully complex characters, spiced liberally with humor."
—*Romantic Times BOOKreviews* on *Barely Behaving*

"This one is hotter than hot!"
—*Romantic Times BOOKreviews* on *Barely Decent*

"Summer not hot enough for you? Pick up this book."
—*The Romance Reader* on *Barely Mistaken*

"Outrageous fun!"
—*Word Wrap* on *Jingle Bell Bride?*

Blaze™

Dear Reader,

Some heroes have a special place in your heart, and Cade Stone is one of those guys for me. He might spend his days tracking down fugitives, but he spends all his time avoiding falling in love. And the more determined he is to avoid it...well, the harder it hits him when he does. Capturing this bounty hunter's heart won't be easy. It's a good thing Sunny Templeton's up to the job.

I loved setting this book in Memphis with its rich history and culture. I have, however, used literary license to create some streets and places that don't exist but seem to fit in with the feel of Memphis. You won't actually find Melvina's or The Best Barbecue, although you'd probably like to stop by for lunch. I've also grown quite attached to the Stone family, whom you can first meet in Rhonda Nelson's November Harlequin Blaze novel, *Feeling the Heat*.

I hope you enjoy Cade and Sunny and their story. I'd love to hear from you. You can visit me at www.jenniferlabrecque.com or contact me snail mail at P.O. Box 298, Hiram, GA 30141.

Happy reading...

Jennifer LaBrecque

JENNIFER LABRECQUE

The Big Heat

TORONTO • NEW YORK • LONDON
AMSTERDAM • PARIS • SYDNEY • HAMBURG
STOCKHOLM • ATHENS • TOKYO • MILAN • MADRID
PRAGUE • WARSAW • BUDAPEST • AUCKLAND

If you purchased this book without a cover you should be aware that this book is stolen property. It was reported as "unsold and destroyed" to the publisher, and neither the author nor the publisher has received any payment for this "stripped book."

ISBN-13: 978-0-373-79371-6
ISBN-10: 0-373-79371-5

THE BIG HEAT

Copyright © 2007 by Jennifer LaBrecque.

All rights reserved. Except for use in any review, the reproduction or utilization of this work in whole or in part in any form by any electronic, mechanical or other means, now known or hereafter invented, including xerography, photocopying and recording, or in any information storage or retrieval system, is forbidden without the written permission of the publisher, Harlequin Enterprises Limited, 225 Duncan Mill Road, Don Mills, Ontario M3B 3K9, Canada.

This is a work of fiction. Names, characters, places and incidents are either the product of the author's imagination or are used fictitiously, and any resemblance to actual persons, living or dead, business establishments, events or locales is entirely coincidental.

This edition published by arrangement with Harlequin Books S.A.

® and TM are trademarks of the publisher. Trademarks indicated with ® are registered in the United States Patent and Trademark Office, the Canadian Trade Marks Office and in other countries.

www.eHarlequin.com

Printed in U.S.A.

ABOUT THE AUTHOR

After a varied career path that included barbecue-joint waitress, corporate number cruncher and bug-business maven, Jennifer LaBrecque found her true calling writing contemporary romance. Named 2001 Notable New Author of the Year and 2002 winner of the prestigious Maggie Award for Excellence, she is also a two-time RITA® Award finalist. Jennifer lives in suburban Atlanta with her husband, an active daughter, one really bad cat, two precocious greyhounds and a Chihuahua who runs the whole show.

Books by Jennifer LaBrecque

HARLEQUIN BLAZE

206—DARING IN THE DARK
228—ANTICIPATION
262—HIGHLAND FLING

HARLEQUIN TEMPTATION

886—BARELY MISTAKEN
904—BARELY DECENT
952—BARELY BEHAVING
992—BETTER THAN CHOCOLATE...
1012—REALLY HOT!

Don't miss any of our special offers. Write to us at the following address for information on our newest releases.

Harlequin Reader Service
U.S.: 3010 Walden Ave., P.O. Box 1325, Buffalo, NY 14269
Canadian: P.O. Box 609, Fort Erie, Ont. L2A 5X3

To Rhonda Nelson. You'll get the dead body call.

1

"SUNNY TEMPLETON needs a decent man," Marlene announced as Cade Stone stepped through the door of AA Atco Bail Bond.

The office manager pinned him with a speculative look, causing Cade to consider turning around and walking right back out. He had no interest in being slotted into the *decent man* role, even if it *was* Sunny Templeton. His brother, Linc, had fallen into that trap and he'd wound up engaged. Not just no, but hell no.

Cade tracked down FTAs—failures to appear—those folks who decided, for whatever reason, to skip their court dates. Once he found them, he hauled them back to jail. They weren't always nice and they were never glad to see him. But if he could handle them, he could certainly handle Marlene…even if she was in matchmaking mode. The glass door finally swung shut behind him, muffling the noise of Memphis traffic along Poplar Street.

"Perfect timing," Linc said with a smirk from where he stood propped in his office doorway.

"Don't look at me," Cade said. "I don't have a decent bone in my body."

"Ha! You've got more decency in your little finger than some people have in their entire body," Marlene said. "Have you seen this?" She waved a flyer at him.

"It's Cecil. He's playing dirty." Linc nodded toward the flyer, looking uncharacteristically sheepish. He held up his hand. "I know. I got us into it and it was a bad idea."

The hair on the back of Cade's neck stood up at the mention of Cecil Meeks, incumbent city council member. Cade possessed excellent people instincts and those instincts had not been happy when he met Cecil. Unfortunately, he hadn't met the man until after Linc had cut a deal to endorse the city councilman in his reelection campaign.

When competition in the form of True Blue American Bail Bonds had moved in down the street, AA Atco's business had taken a sizeable hit. Linc's fiancée, Georgia, had suggested billboard ads featuring Linc and Cade. According to Georgia, they were hot, good-looking guys, and it didn't hurt that they'd brought in top dollar at a bachelor charity auction they'd been roped into the year before last.

Since it was mostly women bailing men out of jail, it didn't take a rocket scientist to follow her reasoning. Unfortunately, with business down, they didn't have the money to buy the billboard space…and that was where Meeks came in.

Cecil Meeks was a media whore whose face was everywhere. And while AA Atco wasn't looking at the political side of it, they definitely needed the exposure. A couple of cable-TV ads and four huge billboards that caught commuter traffic later, they'd gotten it. There had definitely been a change in their bottom line thanks to the publicity. But Cade hadn't liked Cecil from the minute he'd met him. There hadn't been anything specific, just a general dislike and mistrust.

So, Linc's announcement that Cecil was playing dirty didn't surprise Cade in the least.

Unlike Cecil, though, Marlene was good people. She'd been a classy addition to AA Atco when she'd taken on the job of office manager six months prior, following her husband's midlife crisis with a Vegas showgirl and their subsequent divorce.

"Just take a look at this," Marlene said, bristling with outrage.

Cade took the offered sheet of paper. Ever since they'd done the ads with Cecil, Cade had followed the city council race and the candidates. Sunny

Templeton had an impressive record. She'd brought a lot of energy and good ideas to the various committees she'd served on in the past couple of years and was campaigning on the same. As of yesterday she'd pulled slightly ahead of Cecil in the polls.

A red banner across the top of the flyer shouted, *"Do you want this party girl for city council?"* The rest was obviously a page lifted directly from a singles' Web site. A quarter-page picture of a blonde in a bikini holding what appeared to be a mixed drink in her hand smiled at the camera with the most startling, amazing eyes.

At that moment, Cade felt as if he'd just been jolted with a stun gun, the impact ricocheting through him all the way to the soles of his feet in his black flak boots. It was as if she stared straight into him, through him. And every protective instinct he possessed—and that was more than a few—was roused.

"Where'd you get this?" he asked, putting the flyer back on Marlene's desk.

Linc pushed away from the doorjamb. "I met Georgia at the mall during her lunch hour to look at china patterns—"

"China patterns? You were looking at dishes?" Cade stared at Linc. A month ago, the man would've gouged out his eyes before he went to look at *china patterns.*

Linc shrugged nonchalantly. “Hey, if it makes Georgia happy…”

That his brother had been reduced to this was just…sad. Cade was at a loss. His siblings were obviously losing their respective minds. In the span of three months both his sister, Gracie, and Linc had gotten engaged. The office had become damn wedding central.

Lately, too, he’d caught Gracie and Marlene looking at him like his single status was a problem to be solved. No, thanks. He’d stick with the dating rule they’d picked up from their father. Keep it light, keep it simple and never date a woman for more than four weeks.

It wasn’t the wedding part that was so bad, but the falling in love business. Gracie he could almost understand, she’d only been eight when their mother died. But he didn’t know what the hell had happened to Linc. Linc knew better. He’d been twelve, old enough. He’d seen the way their father had been crushed when their mother died in a car accident. If Cade hadn’t stepped up to the plate, God knows what would’ve happened to them while Martin spent three months buried in a bottle. It’d been a harsh lesson that love could damn near destroy you and Cade had tried his best to watch out for Gracie and Linc over the years. All he could do now was shake his head over Linc doing something as stupid as falling in love. He worried about both of them leaving themselves so vulnerable.

"So, you were picking out china at the mall?"

"Yeah. When we finished we found the flyer shoved under the windshield wiper. It was on every car in the parking lot."

"I hope she's got someone in her corner to back her up," Marlene said with a pointed look in Cade's direction.

Despite the fact that Marlene's comment was manipulative, Cade did feel protective. It was his nature. Even though it was damned inconvenient at times, he couldn't even pass a stranded motorist without stopping to help. Plus, he never should've ignored his gut with Meeks. He felt damn guilty that they'd campaigned against Sunny by endorsing Meeks.

"I wish we'd never endorsed him," Marlene said, uncannily echoing his thoughts. "You boys are better than that." At thirty-four and thirty-two, Cade and Linc weren't exactly boys but Marlene liked to refer to them that way and they let her. She pursed her lips. "Do you think he made it up?"

Cade shook his head. "I'm not a Meeks fan but I don't think he wrote it. It'd be too easy for him to get caught."

"How embarrassing for poor Sunny," Marlene said, slanting a look at Cade. "Like I said, she needs a decent man."

The phone rang and Marlene took the call, sparing Cade the need to reply.

He picked up the flyer again and studied it. Shoulder-length blond hair, nice smile, okay figure but nice legs, average height. Not knock-you-down gorgeous but those eyes… And why'd he have a gut-clenching sense of recognition deep inside him?

He shifted from one foot to the other and deliberately looked away from her picture. According to the flyer, her interests were running—that explained the nice legs—stained-glass design and urban revitalization.

Linc looked over his shoulder. "Looks like a nice woman."

"Yep." Attraction—intense, irrational, unwelcome—stabbed at him. "Not my type," Cade added, just to set the record straight. He liked his women laid-back, easy-going. Marlene had used the word *shallow,* which he considered a bit harsh. This woman, despite her easy smile, struck him as intense. No, thanks. Instinct told him she'd be trouble with a capital *T.* "I'm just looking."

"You and every other guy in Memphis," Linc said.

A totally alien, proprietary feeling swamped Cade. What a piss-him-off idea that every other guy in Memphis was looking at her picture and feeling the same feeling of…he didn't even know how to describe it. He just knew he didn't like it.

Linc canted his head to the side. "Those are some nice legs. Not that I'm actually looking, 'cause Georgia would have my ass."

"Yeah? Then maybe you shouldn't look. She might drag you out to pick china patterns again."

"Easy, bro."

"We all have to vote for her," Marlene said, jumping back into the conversation after hanging up the phone. "I, for one, don't appreciate and am not taken in by a smear campaign. Boys?"

Linc threw up his hands. "Hey, I'm there. Count me in."

Cade put the flyer back on Marlene's desk. "Sure. But we might as well piss in the wind. She's screwed."

And in the meantime, he'd make a phone call. He didn't want to get involved and he sure as hell didn't want to meet her, but maybe he could help from behind the scenes.

"WHAT A SPINELESS TOAD," Sunny Templeton fumed.

"If you think you're going to faint, put your head between your knees," Sheila, her mentor, friend and campaign manager instructed.

Sunny stared at the flyer. "I'm not going to faint but my head may very well explode." She sucked in a deep breath, trying to control the temper that occasionally got her in trouble.

"Exploding heads aren't good," Sheila said.

"Nope. And exploding heads don't figure out where to go from here." She rested her head against the steering wheel of her '67 ragtop Mustang and calmed herself. "Actually, I'm not sure whether I'm more angry with him or with me for not anticipating he'd do something like this when I pulled ahead of him."

Well, there was no use sitting in the parking lot of the community center where she'd just made a campaign speech. The stupid flyer had been on every windshield in the parking lot when she and Sheila had left the building.

She cranked the car. It turned over the first time. The body and interior might desperately need restoration but it ran like a dream. The early November sun slanted through the windshield like a soothing balm.

She felt calmer, more rational once again. "We

need a plan. Something more constructive than me suggesting Cecil do something anatomically impossible." Okay, maybe she wasn't totally rational just yet.

"I think the best way to handle it is to ignore it," Sheila said. "Meeks is looking for a reaction and I say we don't give him one."

"Good idea." Sunny nodded her agreement. "This—" she nodded toward the flyer crumpled next to the gearshift "—has nothing to do with the campaign or my qualifications." Her temper escalated all over again. "Can you believe he called me a girl?"

"Of course he did. You're a thirty-year-old successful entrepreneur with a strong civic track record. He's desperate to invalidate you and party girls don't run for city council. He knows people have responded to your sincerity. They know you genuinely care about this city."

Sunny knew that was true. Granted there were some really dirty parts and nobody was naming it the most beautiful city in the U.S., but she loved Memphis with its rich history and diversity. Running for city council wasn't about the power or ego gratification—she sincerely believed she could make a difference. If she thought Cecil would do a better job for the district and the community she never would've stepped up to the plate. "Well, we've run a clean campaign based on the issues. Let's hope voters are turned off by his stunt."

"Sunny?"

"Yeah?"

"Um, I'm not being critical, just curious." Sheila was always so careful not to offend whereas Sunny tended to be much more blunt and plain-spoken. "Why'd you do a singles' ad on the Internet?"

"I guess for the same reasons everyone else does. It offers a much broader base of men to choose from. You can sort of get to know them and if they're creeps, you just don't write back anymore. Plus, since I design Web sites, it just seemed like the natural technology fit for me." It was *mostly* the truth. Sunny offered a rueful laugh. "It never occurred to me that it could come back to bite me in the butt."

"Have you met anyone?"

"Not yet." It was a dismal state romantically—well, sexually, to be more accurate—that she was in.

Speaking of which, she made a right onto Tolliver and caught the red light directly across from the looming billboard.

There he was, Cecil Meeks, unfortunately larger than life, plastered on the billboard for the city, or at least the portion driving by on busy, congested

Tolliver Boulevard, to see. Even more unfortunate, he was flanked by The Bounty-hunting Brothers, as she'd mentally tagged them. Cade and Linc Stone. The caption proclaimed, "We've Got Your Man."

Sheila sighed. "He may be a toad, but he's a smart toad. Those billboards were a good move."

"Yep. Very smart." She thought it was big of her to give credit where credit was due, even if she did despise Cecil Meeks. She hadn't liked Cecil when she'd joined the race. She knew by the end he'd either earn a grudging respect from her or she'd despise him. She was ready to be signed up for the latter.

"Those two looked fully capable of hunting down and hauling back pretty much anyone. Probably over half the female population in the city would do the crime and skip a court date just to have one of those two haul them back," Sheila said, with a semidreamy look on her face. Sunny knew the feeling.

"I'm counting on Memphis women voting with their brains instead of their hormones."

She supposed there were enough women who would find Cade's tawny-eyed, piercing, I'll-kick-your-ass-and-enjoy-doing-it stare sexy, or swoon over Linc's longer hair and devil-may-care smile.

Sunny sniffed and wrapped her fingers tighter around the steering wheel. If you liked those kinds of looks in a man, that was.

She never had. She'd always preferred more intellect than brawn. And those muscle-bound types tended to have control issues and since she liked being in control it was pretty much an oil and water situation. Plus, not long after the billboards went up she'd overheard two campaign volunteers discussing the Stone brothers. Both of them had a reputation for changing women almost as regularly as their underwear.

Which was why it was confounding that she'd developed a *thing* for Cade Stone. Tall and dark with those golden eyes, that sensual, unsmiling mouth and an element of the untamed about him, he'd been a shock to her system from the first time she'd laid eyes on that offensive billboard.

Even now, driving past the image, with Cecil launching his dirty offensive in the campaign's eleventh hour and Sheila riding shotgun in her car, she tingled from head to toe. Heat coursed through her and left her wriggling in her car seat.

It was nutty that she felt such an intense physical, mental, emotional response to a he-man photo...and it was every dang time she drove past. And lately she'd become so...*entangled* that he'd shown up, brimming with muscle and testosterone, in her dreams. She'd imagined his kisses in exquisite detail—his mouth on hers, the scrape of his sexy scruff as he slid his lips down her neck and across her collarbone, the bunching of his muscles beneath her fingertips as she grasped his broad shoulders, the feel of his hands mapping her body. And then she'd wake up, gripped by restlessness, her body humming with arousal. It was just so damn weird to be sexually fixated on someone she'd never met and most likely wouldn't like anyway.

It had been sheer desperation then, that drove her to take out that singles' Web ad. If a man on a billboard could leave her hot and bothered, why not a guy on the Internet?

Unfortunately, none of her Internet dating responses had bumped Cade Stone out of the fantasy hot seat…yet. And that was the part of the truth she'd left out for Sheila. No one else had an inkling that a simple drive-by sighting left her nipples hard and her hoo-ha wet.

She turned right off Tolliver and half a block later bypassed the alley that housed the garage behind her house. She always opted for the on-street parking in the front.

Rats were fond of the back alley and her rodent aversion bordered on phobic. And if the rats gnawed through the Mustang's wiring, she'd be hard-pressed to cough up the bucks to fix it after sinking her savings into her campaign fund. She'd rather jockey for on-street parking any day.

"You know, Sunny, I think this flyer's not going to be a big deal," Sheila said. "People will get it and toss it. I don't think anyone's going to pay a bit of attention."

Sunny turned left onto her street and immediately braked.

She looked at Sheila. "I hope it's true that there's no such thing as bad press—" news vans sat double-parked in front of her row house, midway down the block, which also doubled as her campaign headquarters "—because they've definitely paid attention."

She squared her shoulders. She'd talk to them for a few minutes and then it would be over.

How bad could it be?

2

One month later...

"How are you?" Sheila asked as Sunny settled opposite her onto the familiar hard laminate seat at Melvina's Soul Food.

"I'm starving. How about you?" Sunny inhaled the aroma of collard greens, corn bread and candied yams, ignoring the deeper implication of whether or not she had fully recovered from the debacle following her election loss.

Melvina's soothed her with its juxtaposition of stark but clean concrete floors, laminate seats, bars over the windows and rich comfort food. After the last four weeks of hell—and without being a whiner, it had truly been hellacious—she was getting back on her feet, but her soul could use a healthy dose of culinary comfort.

"I didn't think I was hungry until I smelled the food and now...yeah," Sheila said, leaning across the table a bit to be heard. "And I'll let you slide now, but we're going to talk before lunch is over."

Melvina's was always noisy and today was no exception, with conversation vying with a blues Christmas CD playing over the loudspeaker—Sunny was pretty sure that was Memphis's own Koko Taylor belting out "Have You Heard the News." A thirty-year collection of baby Jesus ornaments adorned a Christmas tree in the middle of the small restaurant. According to Melvina, Jesus was the reason for the season and there wasn't room on her tree for anything else except the star on top.

Melvina herself delivered two sweet teas to the table. "Look at what the cat done drug in," she said with a wide smile. "We sure have missed you."

"Not nearly as much as I've missed y'all." Melvina, her son, TJ, and his wife, Charity, were old friends. She'd known them all since she'd "discovered" Melvina's when she was a University of Memphis student along with TJ and Charity ten years ago.

The older woman gave Sunny a bone-crushing hug—who'd have thought such a small, seemingly frail woman could hug so hard—and Sunny squeezed back.

Melvina and Sheila exchanged greetings and Melvina crossed her arms over her chest, her mouth settling into a disapproving frown. "That was just wrong what that man did to you and wrong what them news folk did after that."

Sunny smiled and shrugged, determined to put it behind her. "It seems to be over now." It wasn't good when the flyers had been spread around town but she'd never dreamed it would explode the way it had. In one of those weird, totally unwelcome quirks of fate, the election and flyer had been picked up by the AP and Reuters and mushroomed into a gargantuan tabloid/Internet nightmare of humiliation. Sunny clad in a bikini had become the election flyer seen around the world. And she'd learned an important lesson. No one ever actually died from humiliation or harassment. She was still-living proof.

Melvina's lips thinned to a hard line. "TJ saw your picture on a late-night TV show." Who in the world *hadn't* would be a shorter list. Sunny, or rather her attendant flyer, had made number three on the *Top Ten Stupid Things To Do When You're Running for Public Office* list. "And Charity saw some stuff on the Internet."

Not hard to imagine since Sunny had been the butt of innumerable jokes circulating on the blogosphere. She'd tried to avoid them, but couldn't help reading each and every one. It was like watching a train wreck—the train wreck that had become her life. She'd thought after a few days of infamy it would die down. That was the way those things worked, right? Wrong. Just when it looked as if things were dying down, it flared back up. But now…four weeks and counting, it finally seemed over. Sunny considered it a minor miracle she'd managed to maintain her dignity and her temper through it all.

"I think it's finally over." No one had pointed or stared at her in at least two days since she'd ventured out of her house once again. No one cheered, jeered or tried to take her picture. No more Web design contracts had cancelled on her except the one. And since she'd disconnected her home phone after changing the number three times in as many weeks, the harassing phone calls had ceased. Her cell number was only available to a select few.

"That Meeks ought to be horse-whipped for starting all this," Melvina declared.

"Too good for him," Sheila opined.

"He'll get his one day," Sunny said. She wasn't sure how or when, but he would. She was ready to get on with her life, but that included settling with Meeks. Revenge would be hers.

Melvina glanced around and lowered her voice.

"Me and TJ, we know people. You want Meeks taken care of, whatever you want, we know people."

"You're a good friend, Melvina. I'll keep that in mind." Having him beat up wasn't what she intended but it was good to know your friends had your back. In a darker, less lucid, PMS moment she *had* fantasized that Meeks's penis would fall off in a very public place and then a group of rogue rabid squirrels would attack him and gnaw his nuts off. However, chocolate had helped and she'd moved on. Now she just wanted the dirt on him she knew was somewhere to be found. She'd been working some contacts, asking around. Patience and perseverance would yield results in the end.

"You just say the word," Melvina said, nodding. "I better get back to the kitchen." She turned, wiping her hands on the ever-present apron knotted around her waist. "I'll send TJ out with corn bread and two vegetable plates."

Melvina hurried off, yelling for her son along the way.

Sunny took a long swallow of the sweet tea. Sheila scraped her nail down the condensation gathered on the outside of her glass. "So things are back to normal?"

"I wouldn't exactly call it normal, but it's not what it has been for the past few weeks."

TJ dropped off a plate of Melvina's corn bread, which was actually fried like a big corn bread pancake, and two pale-aqua melamine plates piled high with collards, candied yams and fried okra. "Enjoy, ladies," he said. "This is on the house."

"But—" Sunny protested.

TJ cut her off. "Hey, I'm the finance whiz with the college degree, remember?" He winked at her. "I say Melvina's can afford to comp a couple of friends now and then."

The last month had severely frazzled her nerves and pushed her to the edge, but TJ's offer made her teary-eyed. She sucked it up. If she hadn't cried then, she darn sure wasn't going to lose it now. "Thanks, TJ."

He smiled, "Just enjoy it, okay?" He moved on to the next table with his laden tray.

"That was nice," Sheila said.

"Very." Her mouth watering in anticipation, Sunny broke off a crispy edge of the corn bread and popped it into her mouth. Heavenly.

"I wanted to wait until the dust settled but have you given any thought to what you're going to do next? You aren't going to just go to ground, are you?"

"No. I'll continue my committee work." She'd thought about it a lot. It'd be easy to just toss in the towel but the easy thing to do wasn't necessarily the right thing to do. Even though it meant working with Cecil, she wasn't giving up her committee work. "If I quit altogether then Cecil's really won."

"Atta girl," Sheila said with an encouraging smile.

And honestly she was sick and tired of Cecil Meeks and his fiasco consuming her life. The worst of it was that Cecil hadn't won because he was the better candidate. If she believed he'd do his job properly, all of this wouldn't really matter. Well, that was a lie. It'd matter but she'd feel better about him being in office.

She took a deep breath. She wanted to talk about something else, think about something else. She'd much rather talk about Sheila and Dan's twentieth-anniversary trip to Key West. They were flying out as soon as Dan finished work today. Monday struck her as an odd time to leave but apparently the hotel offered a discounted Monday to Monday package. "You all packed for Florida?"

"I've *been* packed. I can't wait. One glorious week of sun, snorkeling and boinking my husband senseless. And not necessarily in that order."

As far as Sunny could tell, Sheila and Dan, both in their mid-forties, had their moments like any other couple, but unlike many others, they still seemed to genuinely enjoy one another's company in and out of the bedroom. It was the kind of relationship she'd like to have one day, if she ever stumbled across Mr. Right.

Sunny laughed. "I'd opt for nearly senseless. He'll be useless if he's senseless."

"Nah. He's a man. The two brains operate independently." Sheila smiled like the cat with the canary. "At least I hope so because he's guaranteed to lose his mind." She leaned across the table and dropped her voice, even though none of the other customers were paying them any attention. "Did I tell you about the package I shipped ahead?"

"Honestly, if you did, I don't remember with everything that's been going on. Do tell."

"I wasn't sure about getting it through security at the airport, so I shipped a toy box to the hotel."

"A toy box?" Sunny was pretty sure she knew where Sheila was going.

Sheila leaned farther across the table, barely avoiding sticking her boob into her yams, and lowered her voice. "I ordered a selection of sex toys online. A couple of outfits for me. A couple for him. Some gels, some lotions, a collection of body jewelry and a couple of other inventive things." She sat back with a wicked smile.

Sunny laughed, her imagination running with that scenario, casting herself and her billboard man in the starring roles. At this point, the only way to get over her thing for Cade Stone required either professional help or to seriously get laid. Sure he had that I-can-rock-your-world-baby look, but he also had that I'm-in-charge look and after growing up with her overbearing parents, Sunny didn't need anyone else in charge of her. Ever.

"I want him to know that twenty years doesn't mean things have to be boring."

"Have things gotten boring?" she asked as Sheila munched corn bread. Sheila gave her the wait-a-minute-while-I-chew-and-swallow-my-food sign, so Sunny sampled the yams.

She'd been there, done that, got the T-shirt for boring sex. *Maybe it's because you always pick men you can push around,* an annoying little voice whispered inside her.

Sheila took a sip of tea. "Not exactly boring. Maybe a little routine. Proactive is better than reactive."

"I'm sure Dan will enjoy your proactive stance. You don't need for me to look after your plants while you're gone or check the mail or anything?" Sheila had done so much for her, giving advice and time freely, Sunny wanted to do something in return.

"Dan's cousin's got it covered." Dan's cousin would spend the next week refinishing the hardwood floors in their house and remodeling the bathroom while they were gone. "The only thing you need to look after is yourself. Are you sure you're okay? I've been worried about you." Sheila shot her an admonishing look. "And you know I would've dragged you to the Kincaids' with us last week if I'd known you were staying home alone on Thanksgiving."

Sunny grinned. "Which is precisely why I didn't mention it. I was infinitely happier at home working on my wolf than enduring another round of disapproval and I-told-you-so's at the Templeton family table."

Actually, working on her stained-glass wolf had kept her sane and grounded in the last month. It had given her a creative outlet to focus on and lose herself in. She smiled to herself. Her wolf had stood guard for her, against the rest of the world. Her, her semiconstructed stained-glass wolf, and a take-out dinner from her grocer's deli had suited her Thanksgiving just fine. Traipsing along to Shelia's in-laws' during a family holiday or intruding on any of her other friends hadn't felt right.

"I just don't get your family. They drive me crazy." Poor Sheila. They did drive her crazy. It frustrated Sheila that Sunny's parents and her sister, Nadine, weren't more supportive. It didn't particularly bother Sunny anymore. She'd moved beyond needing their approval years ago, which was a damn good thing, all things considered.

They disapproved of her job as a Web designer—no stability in computer-related self-employment, according to her dad. They disdained the row house she'd bought as an investment in a rundown section of the city on the edge of revitalization. According to them, a new cookie-cutter house in a cookie-cutter subdivision was what she should've bought as a surer return on her money. Actually, in their book, marrying an accountant the way her sister, Nadine, had was the real bankable investment. They considered Sunny's volunteer work a waste of time. And they'd never understood her running for city council since they'd been sure she'd lose to Cecil Meeks.

"Please tell me they've risen to the occasion during all of this," Sheila said.

Sunny shrugged. "They've been embarrassed."

"I can read between those lines."

Growing up, she'd been the odd man out, determined even as a child to walk her own path. Her overbearing parents, however, had never embraced her independence, spontaneity or free thinking. "Remember the Pearls of Wisdom. It is what it is."

"Okay, okay. I'm letting it go based on the Pearls of Wisdom."

The summer she'd been ten, they'd moved and her life had changed. Despite their disparate ages, she'd found a kindred spirit in an elderly widow next door. Mrs. Pearl had spent a lifetime studying Native Americans and particularly the Chickasaw of western Tennessee.

Sunny had spent hours in Mrs. Pearl's backyard and at her kitchen table absorbing Native American culture and developing a deep and abiding love for nature and community.

Sunny had been particularly fascinated by and seemed to have a gift for understanding and identifying animal totems, her own and others. On Sunny's twelfth birthday, Mrs. Pearl had given her a hummingbird ring—the hummingbird being Sunny's animal totem. Sunny treasured the simple sterling-silver design of a hummingbird drinking from a flower. Her long-standing favorite piece of jewelry, she'd resized it twice as she'd grown and always wore it on her right hand.

Mrs. Pearl had exerted the most influence in shaping Sunny's life. She'd helped her move beyond her need for her parents' approval, teaching her to embrace who and what she was, and likewise accepting her parents in the same vein. It was a gift Sunny had carried with her into adulthood even though the dear woman had died during

Sunny's junior year in college. She'd dubbed Mrs. Pearl's life lessons *Pearls of Wisdom,* and she'd shared them with Sheila on several occasions.

She sure didn't want Shelia worrying about her on her anniversary trip. "Go. Have a good time. I'm fine." She was done wallowing in this disaster. From here on she was employing positive thinking. "The worst is behind me, now it's smooth sailing."

"ANY NEWS YET?" Cade propped the phone against his shoulder as he leaned back in his near-ancient office chair.

"I've had a couple of leads that wound up to be dead ends. Meeks is a slippery guy," said Danny Jones, the private eye Cade had contacted the day Sunny Templeton's flyer had hit. Every once in a while he and Linc needed a little private eye help, and Danny was their go-to man—one of the best in the business. If there was dirt, Danny'd dig it up. "It's been a month. Want me to give it a rest?"

"Nope. Stay on it. Sooner or later he'll slip or something will turn up."

"You're the boss. I'll touch base with you next week."

"Good deal."

He hung up and found Linc leaning against his door frame. "Did you sic Jones on Meeks?"

"He's just doing a little digging."

Linc grinned. "You couldn't stand it, could you?"

Cade shrugged. "Just nosing around." His brother knew him as well as anyone. And no, it was genetically impossible for him to sit around and do nothing to help Sunny Templeton when he felt responsible for aiding and abetting Meeks in defeating her. His guilt and sense of responsibility had escalated with every incident reported in the paper, on the Internet, and each damned late-night show.

And honest to God, she was driving him crazy. She'd looked like trouble the first time he'd seen that damn flyer. How he felt about her was…complicated…which was stupid considering he'd never met her, didn't want to meet her. He'd found it impossible to toss that sheet of paper. Instead he'd stuck it in his desk. Every time he opened his drawer and saw it, something inside him shifted. He didn't like things shifting inside him. He ought to just toss it but he couldn't quite make himself do it. Sunny Templeton had become a phantom PITA—a real Pain In The Ass.

The sooner Jones found something on Meeks, and his gut told him there was something to be found, the sooner he could turn it over to Sunny Templeton to use and then wash his hands of her. *Then* he'd toss the flyer.

"By the way, Georgia wanted me to remind you that you need to stop by the formal wear shop to be fitted for the tux. My best man's got to be jam up on the big day and she says we big boys are gonna require special orders."

Okay, once upon a time he and Linc had known one another well but his brother in love was something of a stranger at times. Linc was yet another cautionary tale in Cade's life. *This* was what love reduced men to. He was tempted to ask Linc if he still actually had a dick but that would only piss him off. Instead Cade stood and stretched. "Yeah, I'll get by there sometime this week."

"I'll let Georgia know," Linc said, wandering back to his office, doubtless to call Georgia.

Cade supposed if Linc had to be an idiot in love at least he'd chosen well. Cade liked Georgia. He also liked Gracie's fiancé well enough. He grabbed the paperwork on his latest FTA apprehension off his desk and walked it out to Marlene.

"Thanks," she said, without looking up from the computer monitor. "You know, I'm thinking about signing up for one of those online dating things."

Cade shook his head. *That* was random. Had he just heard her correctly? "Did you say online dating?"

"Yeah. You know, one of those Internet matchmaking things."

He had heard right.

"The hell you say!" Martin bellowed from his office. Apparently his father had heard, as well. Great. Martin stomped out to join them, a bottled Coke in his hand. At six foot six he stood two inches taller than Cade and still didn't carry an ounce of spare flesh. "What's wrong with you, woman?"

Marlene merely quirked an eyebrow at Martin's outburst. "I'm ready for some excitement. All my friends want to introduce me to boring men."

Linc strolled out of his office. He didn't like to miss out on anything.

Marlene eyed all of them. "What? We're not exactly overrun with eligible men walking through the door here. Online dating seems a reasonable vetting process. I want excitement, romance." Martin started to smirk. "I want to get remarried," she tacked on the final installment. Cade's cringe echoed Martin's.

Had everyone lost their minds? Between Linc and Georgia and Gracie and Mark and all the wedding mumbo jumbo floating around the office, Marlene had got caught up in it.

Linc shook his head. "You got rid of one rat-bastard husband. What are you thinking, Marlene?"

Maybe Linc wasn't as far gone as Cade had thought. He did still have an ounce of sense left.

"I'm not cut out for one-night stands. I'm not a love 'em and leave 'em kind of woman. But I have to tell you boys, I miss sex."

Martin snorted his swallow of Coke through his nose, choking and coughing. "Now I know you're one can shy of a six-pack if you want to get remarried so you can have sex."

Cade disagreed with Martin more often than not. In fact, they'd coexisted in an uneasy truce the past twenty years since Cade's mother died, but he had to throw his towel in with the old man on this one.

Marlene shot Martin a withering look. "It's the way I'm made. Some of us aren't emotionally or mentally built to indulge in casual sex."

An uncomfortable silence filled the room except for the ticking of the big wall clock. It had worked well enough for three of the four of them present.

Cade spoke up. "If you're going to do this online dating thing, promise me you won't go out with anyone until we approve them." He crossed his arms over his chest. She hadn't done such a good job with the first husband and there were some real pieces of crap out there. Someone had to make sure she didn't strike out if she was determined to go round two. And Marlene might not be family, but she worked for him and no one screwed with anyone under his domain unless they wanted a serious ass-kicking.

Linc nodded. "Good plan. We can make sure you don't hook up with any creeps."

Marlene looked from him to Linc and back. "Fine. You boys can approve them."

"And I'll help you put together your Web page," Martin announced.

"I don't need any help putting it together."

"Sure you do. You want to make sure you don't put out any casual sex signals and I know all of those." Martin crossed his arms over his chest in a perfect imitation of Cade. "I know what men your age are looking for."

"But I don't want a man like you," Marlene shot back with a sweet smile.

Linc raised an eyebrow at Cade and Cade answered with a faint shrug. Martin's scowl deepened. Was Martin's scowl more territorial than protective? Cade hoped the hell not.

Martin and Marlene would be a disaster. Once Martin had pulled himself up by his bootstraps after Lucy's death, he'd taken up serial dating. Martin liked women and he treated them with respect, but he made sure they never got too close.

Marlene wasn't the kind of woman who'd go for

the four-week wooing she'd get from Martin. Plus she was damn good at what she did and they didn't need to lose her when things went south at week five.

Martin gritted his teeth. "Then I'll put down the opposite of everything I'd look for in a woman."

"That might work then," Marlene shot back. She looked at the three of them, ringing her desk. "If I pass out from the overdose of testosterone in here, someone just drag me out to the sidewalk."

Marlene promptly ignored them, returning to the computer screen, humming that old seventies tune "Love is in the Air."

Cade headed for the door. He was getting the hell out before he caught whatever was going around. He'd rather face down hardened criminals than get caught up in this love business.

3

SUNNY SANG ALONG with Lena Horne's "Stormy Weather," her radio set to classic jazz, on her way to the grocery store after lunch. The remainder of her meal was packed in a to-go box next to her but her kitchen at home was dismally empty. Taking advantage of being alone in the car, she sang louder. Sunny couldn't carry a tune in a bucket, but she loved to sing. Sometimes when she sang at home, the cat next door yowled.

She felt better than she had in days. No, make that weeks. She'd run a gamut of emotions—depressed, pissed, violated, humiliated. Yep, that about summed it up. But now she felt good. No, make that great.

Despite the rain clouds gathering overhead, she was setting her personal course for nothing but sunny skies from here on out.

She pulled up to the four-way stop at Jackson and Hull Streets. A man in a Santa suit stood on the corner, ringing a bell, holding a donation can for a local food bank. Blue car went. The car to her left should go next.

Her head whipped around in a double-take. No. Was she hallucinating? It couldn't be. It was.

Cecil Meeks sat at the stop sign on her left in his shiny, black, chrome-trimmed, late-model Cadillac DeVille. All the emotions she thought she'd processed and worked through in the past four weeks swamped her.

She sucked in a deep breath aimed at calming. Problem was she didn't feel calm. *Hold on to your temper, hold on to your temper, hold on to your temper,* she silently chanted.

Meeks spotted her and the son of a bitch actually smirked. Full, in-your-face smirking, despite the fact that he was in one car and she in another. She sucked another lungful of air in on the one before, determined to be the bigger person but it didn't seem to help.

His turn to drive.

Meeks accelerated and waved. And laughed.

He'd made an international laughingstock of her and now he was laughing in her face. One second she was sitting there, the next she just… floored it.

Bam. Her Mustang plowed into the rear door of

his Caddie, the impact jerking her against the seat belt. She didn't have an airbag to go off, but her horn did.

She sat there. She'd just rammed Meeks's car… with hers.

He jumped out of his car, screaming and waving a cell phone but she couldn't hear him over the blaring of her horn. Stunned by her own behavior, she sat and stared at him. Unfortunately, his penis didn't fall off in the street and no rabid squirrels came running. She did, however, hear the approaching wail of a police siren.

Santa wrenched her door open, his beard askew, his bell still in his hand. "Are you okay? Are you trapped in your car?"

She unbuckled her seat belt, her hand amazingly steady even though she felt as if she were shaking all over. "I'm fine."

She climbed out, her legs barely holding her upright.

"Hey, aren't you the lady—" he looked over at Cecil jumping up and down like a maggot on a stick "—isn't he—"

"I am. He is."

Suddenly the clouds opened up and it started to pour. Not the soft gentle rain of a summer shower but a cold, driving, early-December deluge that stung.

Sunny tilted her face upward. Maybe she'd just drown before things got any worse. If she was lucky.

Luck, however, didn't seem to be running her way.

"WHAT IN THE HELL was Sunny Templeton thinking?" Cade muttered to himself as he watched the five o'clock news's lead story over Marlene's shoulder on her computer monitor.

Meeks had a bandage wrapped around his head and a sling supported his right arm as he played to the camera. "It was terrifying. I didn't recognize her until I drove past. It was the rage and hate filling her eyes that caught my attention and then the next thing I knew she attacked me with her vehicle. She clearly tried to kill me. I'm lucky I walked away with only the injuries I sustained."

"Is this your first interaction with Ms. Templeton since the election?" the reporter asked.

"Mercifully, yes. And I hope my last. The woman's definitely deranged."

The female reporter quirked her eyebrow. "Some people believe you crossed the line when your campaign put out that flyer."

Cecil adopted a sanctimonious demeanor. "Absolutely not. I considered that a public service. When you put yourself up for public office, there can be no distinction between public and private life. The public had a right to know what they were getting with Ms. Templeton."

The reporter faced the camera. "Ms. Templeton is currently being held at the Memphis Police Department pending bail. We'll bring you updates as available. Back to you now, Gretchen."

The camera cut back to the in-studio news anchor and Cade filtered out the rest, his attention still focused on Sunny Templeton and Cecil Meeks.

"That man ought to be ashamed," Marlene said, switching to another screen with one click of her mouse in evident disgust. "I'm sorry we had anything to do with him."

Cade straightened. "That makes two of us. Meeks is a worm. It'd be kind of funny that she wrecked his new Cadillac, if it hadn't landed her in jail."

Marlene sighed. "I'd go over there and help her if I could." Marlene had turned Sunny into a regular Joan of Arc in the last month. He'd be hard-pressed to believe Sunny Templeton had a more staunch supporter anywhere in Memphis than Marlene. "I'm sure True Blue will handle the bond." She shot him a look that made the tiny hairs on the back of his neck quiver. "It's a shame. I think she's a nice girl. Pretty. Smart. Nice figure in a bikini."

"Don't look at me that way." Marlene might've decided to look for love in all the wrong places herself but she could leave him out of her matchmaking schemes. She'd considered herself the matchmaker extraordinaire when Linc and Georgia had wound up together. She was barking up the wrong tree, however, with him and Sunny Templeton.

"I'm not looking at you any way."

"Yes, you are." His single-man-in-danger-of-being-fixed-up alarm was going off.

"You're paranoid."

"Go figure," he said. Marlene obviously had decided in her single-minded brain that Sunny was the woman for him. Not by a long shot. God help him if Marlene ever got wind that he'd put Jones onto Meeks to dig up dirt for the woman sitting across the street in a jail cell.

Unfortunately, Marlene could ride this for hours. Fortunately it was time for him to head home. He wanted a nice dinner and a glass of wine or a cold beer.

"I'm outta here. If you're through, I'll walk you to your car," he said. The upside to their location was they were right across from the jail. The downside to their location...they were right across from the jail. Yeah, that meant a bunch of cops were around, but it also meant a lot of slime was around. Throughout the years, they'd made it a habit for one of them to always accompany the office manager to her car.

Marlene unplugged the miniature Christmas tree she'd insisted on buying for her desk corner but left the chili-pepper lights outlining the front window turned on. She'd turned AA Atco into the most festive bail bond office on Poplar Street—hell, probably the entire city of Memphis.

"Let me get my coat," she said.

"You can go ahead, Cade," Martin called out from his office. "I've got a couple of things to go over with Marlene. I'll walk her to her car."

"Thoughtful," Cade said in a sarcastic aside to Marlene. Martin knew what time she left. Why wait until it was time for her to leave to go over things?

"I heard that," Martin groused.

"Good. Remember she's been here all day and she's supposed to go home now," Cade said, stopping by Martin's office door. Martin wasn't the most thoughtful employer. Come to think of it, Martin wasn't thoughtful. Period.

"I'll take her to dinner to cover the overtime. Happy? And I'll help her with that Web page."

What was Martin up to? "Only if Marlene wants dinner." Cade looked at Marlene. "You want dinner?"

"Sure." Marlene's smile was just a tad too honey-sweet. "There's a new sushi place I've been wanting to try."

Cade grinned at Marlene's neat turn of the table and Martin's look of disgust.

"I was thinking something with real food."

Marlene leveled a guileless look at Martin and Cade made for the door. The two of them would figure it out. He had a feeling Martin would dine on sushi tonight. Marlene could be relentless.

Before he reached the door, the jingle bell wreath on the glass jangled as a woman stepped inside. Average height. Dark hair. He'd guess early to mid-thirties. There was something vaguely familiar about her. Cade never forgot a face, which came in very handy in his line of work, but he couldn't quite place this woman.

The woman looked at Marlene. "Hello. I'm Nadine Axmoor. My sister is Sunny Templeton and I need to post bail for her. I've never done this. I have no idea what I'm supposed to do."

That's why he recognized her. There was a family resemblance in the chin and the line of her jaw.

Marlene's mouthed gaped for about two seconds before she recovered her usual aplomb. "Sure. You know that we're the company that campaigned with Cecil Meeks. Are you sure you want to go with us?"

"Marlene," Martin bellowed from his office, "just do it."

"It doesn't matter." The woman waved a dismissive hand. "You're right across from the jail and I need to get this taken care of." She shrugged. "I didn't vote for her, either."

What the hell? Cade's hackles rose. She didn't vote for her own sister? With family like her, who needed enemies like Meeks?

Marlene's lips tightened into a thin disapproving line but she efficiently processed the paperwork. She slid the bond form across the desk to the Axmoor woman who stared at it as if was a snake. "What do I do with that?"

Marlene looked back at her as if Nadine Axmoor were something stuck on the bottom of Marlene's shoe. "You take it across the street and the officer at the front desk will tell you what you need to do from there to get Sunny out."

Nadine pushed the paper back across the desk with one manicured finger. "Oh, no. I have to meet my husband for dinner. It's a business affair with some of his associates. I'm already running late. And have you seen the media waiting on her across the street?" Cade glanced out the front window into the burgeoning twilight. Sure enough, media vans lined the street in front of the jail. "I've gone to the trouble to come down and post bail. I'm done. Sunny got herself into this mess. She can figure it out. Maybe she'll learn to think things through."

Every protective instinct in him surged. He barely bit back a growl of disapproval.

What. A. Bitch.

"We'll handle it from here," Marlene said, standing, practically shoving the other woman out the front door. "If you hurry, maybe you can avoid the worst of rush-hour traffic."

Cade didn't catch the woman's closing comment on the way out, but he had no trouble hearing Marlene once the sister was down the sidewalk. "What a hideous, odious woman." She brushed her hands together. "Good riddance."

"She was a piece of work," Cade agreed.

"Poor Sunny." Marlene inclined her head toward the melee of reporters across the street. "They're going to eat her alive." She very pointedly stared at Cade.

Sunny did need help. He nominated Marlene. "You've got your wish. You can go over there and bail her out."

"No, I can't. You just heard your father ask me to work late."

He was doing what he could on the private-eye front with Danny Jones. That was enough. "Sunny Templeton is not my problem."

"Who would you call to bail you out if you landed in jail?"

"First off, I wouldn't be stupid enough to land in jail—" Marlene cut him off with a look. "Okay, okay. Linc. I'd call Linc. And if I couldn't get him I'd call Gracie. If I couldn't get those two, I'd call you. And after those three strikes I'd be dialing Martin."

"And do you think any of us would leave you to make your way through those sharks waiting outside?"

"I'd lay money Martin might." He didn't count on Martin for shit.

"Watch it, boy," Martin grumbled, but it lacked any real thunder. They both knew there was too much truth backing Cade's words. Martin, his father, the man who should be his staunchest advocate, wasn't altogether a sure thing.

"Sorry, Martin. I call 'em the way I see 'em."

"He wouldn't." There was a quiet firmness, a surety about Marlene's simple statement. "I think he'd lead the way for you, carve a path between them for you. No one that you called would leave you to face that alone." Okay. Okay. "That woman that just walked out of here was the best Sunny

Templeton had to call and that's just plain sad." Unfortunately, that was true. "You're on your way out anyway. It'll take ten, maybe fifteen extra minutes out of your day to handle the bail." She examined the fingernails on her right hand. "Linc says you've got Jones looking for something on Meeks."

Dammit to hell. Linc had a big mouth.

Every internal radar he possessed was going off. Sunny Templeton would be trouble. He knew it. He was working behind the scenes, doing what he could to fix the fact that he'd gone along with Cecil when all his instincts said he shouldn't.

"You know she needs you," Marlene said softly.

The instinct to protect her was even stronger than his instinct of self-preservation. That was his undoing. He couldn't just walk out the door and leave her hanging. He'd go get her out. But it didn't mean he had to like it.

He held out his hand for the paperwork. Marlene beamed at him but didn't relinquish the form. Instead she pointed toward the back closet with the paperwork. "You might want to grab a jacket and take it with you for her. The temperature's dropped about twenty degrees since mid-afternoon. There's a cold front moving in."

Between him, Linc and Martin, there were always a couple of extra jackets in the closet.

Mostly because they just wound up leaving them at work, but sometimes they came in handy as a disguise.

"Fine, I'll grab her a jacket. Go ahead and call a cab and have it waiting around the back. That'll at least avoid most of the melee out front."

A fine frown settled between Marlene's arched brows. "A cab? But—" she glanced at the pink copy of duplicate paperwork on her desk "—I think this address is only a block or two out of your way. Weren't you heading home? Seems like it shouldn't be a big deal to just drop her off on your way."

"Will you be happy then? Will I have thoroughly atoned for my sin? Will you finally concede Sunny Templeton's not my problem?" And would he finally feel as if he could walk away with a clear conscience? That he'd done his best by her?

"Yes. Mostly. Maybe."

He sighed and crossed the room to the back closet. He dug out a well-worn orange and white University of Tennessee jacket from Linc's college days. He also snagged a ball cap off the top shelf.

"Feel free to nominate me for sainthood when I'm through."

Marlene smiled sweetly and passed him the paperwork. Martin snorted from his office. Cade paused in the doorway on his way out. "Enjoy the sushi dinner," he said, closing the door on Marlene's laugh and Martin's grumbling.

The wind held a sharp edge and carried the smell of old grease and hickory smoke from the barbecue shack on the corner. Cade avoided a wadded fast-food bag blowing down the sidewalk and rounded the corner of the building to the small, potholed parking lot beside AA Atco.

He just wanted to get this over with. Done.

He unlocked his car and tossed the jacket and cap onto the passenger seat. Marlene was right, he could take fifteen minutes out of his day to do the woman a good turn. He cranked his car and pulled past the media to an unlit corner of the parking lot close to the back entrance.

He was about to encounter Sunny Templeton in the flesh. No flyer. No newspaper article. No Internet blog. His heart pounded the way it hadn't since he'd apprehended his first skip sixteen years ago.

He had to get a grip. He brought in hardened criminals, for chrissakes. Just how much trouble could it be to bail Sunny Templeton out and drop her off at home?

4

"SHE'S ALL YOURS," officer Jack Winslett, per his name badge, said, speaking over Sunny's shoulder.

Time to face Nadine. It wouldn't be pleasant but it couldn't be any worse than what she'd been through so far. She turned, expecting her sister. Instead she came face-to-face, well to be technically accurate, face-to-wall-of-hard-muscular-chest with the big, badass bounty hunter himself who'd been starring front and center in her secret fantasies. Cade Stone.

She must truly be off the deep end because she locked gazes with his piercing tawny eyes and something primitive, something hot and wild and deliciously disturbing shook her to her core, despite having just been bailed out of jail. More than likely, she was just flat-out disturbed. This hadn't exactly been her finest day. She was tired. Hungry. Grubby. Still damp from her soaking. And to top it off, she'd been hit on by a big woman named Spanky with a skull tattoo on her forearm. And much as he might show up in her fantasies, she didn't want to deal with him in real life. Especially not when she looked like she'd just crawled through hell and back. Feeling flushed and breathless and slightly weak-kneed was downright inconvenient right now.

"What are *you* doing here?" she said, also reminding herself he was the enemy. He'd campaigned for Cecil, against her. He had a lot of nerve showing up here.

A flicker of…remorse, amusement…something flickered in his eyes and then was gone. "I'm passing along your get-out-of-jail card."

His voice was deep, sexy with an underlying hint of gravel. Oh. Sweet. Mother. She reached behind her and grabbed the edge of the desk. A part of her would've been relieved if he'd sounded like Tweety Bird. She was pretty sure she wouldn't be feeling this incredible surge of sexual energy if the guy sounded like he'd just sucked on a helium balloon. That would've killed the fantasy. But no, Cade Stone had to sound as good as he looked.

"You want to take this somewhere else, folks?" Officer Winslett scowled at them. "You're blocking my desk and I've got other people to process."

Cade grasped her by her elbow, his touch

sending another heat wave through her, and led her out into the corridor.

Once outside the release room, she dug in her heels and shook his hand off of her arm. She wanted some answers and his touch was…well, it made coherent thoughts other than "I'd like to see you naked" difficult.

She tilted her head back to look at him. Way back. He had to be nearly a foot taller than her. Fine lines radiated from the corners of eyes that were a golden brown with flecks of black. No-nonsense lines bracketed his mouth. A dark stubble shadowed his jaw. His dark hair was close-cropped. Faint lines etched his forehead. His nose, Romanesque, skewed slightly to one side, as if it'd been broken once or twice and never quite made it back to the center. He was beautiful in a rugged, untamed kind of way.

His size alone would have made him intimidating, but a body-hugging black T-shirt tucked into black jeans, black leather jacket and black military-style boots only furthered the intimidation factor. No one would mistake him for a gentle giant. He seemed hard through and through, but she didn't sense any cruelty, just determination and focus.

She stared him in the eyes, not wanting him to think he intimidated her.

"I don't understand why you're here. I called my sister."

Nadine had been the lesser of two evils. Calling Sheila hadn't been a remote possibility. She wasn't screwing up the woman's vacation. As for calling her other friends, it didn't seem right to drag them into the financial matter of bailing her out. Nadine had plenty to say about Sunny landing herself in jail. Eventually, however, after she'd had her say, she'd agreed to bail her out. So where the heck was she?

Overhead, a fluorescent bulb that needed replacing flickered. She looked away from Cade to an officer escorting a disheveled middle-aged man in handcuffs down the hall.

"Your sister posted your bond but she couldn't make it over here to finish up." Was that a hint of disapproval behind that implacable stare? He'd campaigned for Cecil Meeks. He didn't have room to disapprove of anyone. Then it suddenly occurred to her…color her slow what with being arrested and booked.

"Nadine came to *you* to bail me out?" She could handle her sister's tirades, her disapproval. She could handle Nadine not bothering to show up and give her a ride home. But to have gone to this man's company, the very people who'd been on that billboard with Meeks to post her bond, *that* stung like an open-handed slap to the face.

"Our office is right across the street."

She lifted her chin and started down the hall. "Thanks," she said, more of a dismissal than an actual appreciation. She walked toward the exit arrow at the end of the hall.

He caught up with her easily. "Look, put on this jacket and cap. We'll duck out the back door and I'll give you a lift home."

She hadn't even noticed the items he held in one hand. "No, thank you."

"There are camera crews and news vans outside that are going to crawl all over you when you walk out of here."

Sunny stopped. Cade stopped, too. What did it take to get rid of this man? "Look. I know my sister stuck you with coming over here and bailing me out. I'm bailed. You're done. Go home. Shoo."

Okay, so maybe the accompanying shooing motion was a bit much. Cade Stone didn't look like a man who got shooed very often…uh, probably never. And from the way he narrowed his eyes and thinned his lips, he wasn't happy with it happening now.

"There's nothing I'd like to do more. I'm trying to go home. I just need to take you home on my way."

"That's not happening. How do I know you're not a pervert who just wants to get me in his car?"

After a stunned moment he laughed. If he was a pervert, he was a most amused one. "Sorry to disappoint you, honey, but you're not my type." He rubbed his hand over his head. "Look. I'm just trying to help you out, here."

"The same way you helped me out by campaigning with Cecil? No thanks." She crossed her arms over her chest. Nice to know she wasn't his type. He might have some bone-melting physical effect on her but he wasn't her type, either. Case in point, she'd told him to go away and he was still here. She wasn't feeling particularly tactful. "I don't need your *help,* so quit bugging me."

"I'm *bugging* you—" uh-huh, he didn't like that word any better than he liked *shoo* "—because our secretary has taken you up as the cause of the day. Marlene damn near considers you Joan of Arc. Your sister showing up today and then leaving you high and dry was just icing on the cake. Marlene has taken it into her head that I need to give you a ride home to atone for our sin of being part of Meeks's campaign. If I let you walk out of that door and allow the media to swamp you, if I don't deliver you safely to your door, my life isn't going to be worth living."

She'd lived on her own for the past twelve years. Aside from having been taken into custody today and subsequently released, *she* was the only one that made the decision on whether she walked out of a door or not. "If *you* let me walk out the door…? You're seriously confused on several issues."

"I just know my ass is gonna be grass and Marlene's gonna be the lawnmower."

Maybe she was verging on hysteria because it suddenly struck her as hysterically funny that Mr. Macho Bounty Hunter was angsting over whether this Marlene was pleased or not. "Didn't you say this woman was your secretary? Doesn't that mean she works for you? Yet, you're telling me she's bullying you into taking me home."

He grimaced. "You'd have to know Marlene."

She smirked. "I bet I'd like her."

"I'm sure the two of you would have a regular Mutual Admiration Society going. Now, can I please take you home so I can go home?" He smiled and Sunny was pretty sure that all her insides melted. Thankfully her legs still worked. "Pretty please, with sugar on top." It was much, much better for her peace of mind when he didn't smile. She could actually think when he didn't smile. He should not smile all the time. And she could feel her resolve weakening, crumbling in the face of that sexy, lopsided curl of his mouth.

Where was her pride? Her brain? Her cherished independence? She squared her shoulders. "You know I'm not afraid to go out there and face them."

"No. You don't appear to be. I, however, am afraid to face Marlene. And I'm hungry to boot. Could we just go?" Another rueful flash of faintly crooked teeth, which was somehow all the more appealing than if he'd possessed perfectly aligned pearly whites.

Sunny weighed her options. She didn't owe him anything. He'd campaigned for Cecil and there was a part of her that would enjoy knowing her refusal left him in bad graces with the much-feared Marlene. And she was perversely annoyed at his proclamation that she wasn't his type. Which was just fine because he wasn't her type. Just because her heart was going rat-a-tat-tat didn't mean jack.

She shook her head. "I can't help you with that."

His smile took on a hard edge. "Listen, lady. We can do this my way or we can do this your way. Either way, I'm taking you home."

She needed a bath and dinner and she wouldn't

mind a beer and not necessarily in that order, but his sheer effrontery boggled her mind. She simply had to ask. “And what, pray tell, is your way?”

He sighed. “We’ve been over this part before. You put on the cap and jacket and we walk out the back door.”

“Of course, how stupid of me. It just seems to be *my* way that I’m in the dark about.”

He seemed impervious to her sarcasm. “Well, your way, since you’re unwilling to go under your own power, means I toss you over my shoulder and carry you out the back.”

“You’re kidding.”

“Do I look like I’m kidding?”

“You can’t manhandle me. We’re in a police station. You can’t carry me around like a piece of luggage just because you want to.”

“I just bailed you out on an assault felony. It’s not going to look too good on your part if we go this route.”

“I’ll tell one of the cops.”

“I know I’m being redundant, but these guys know me. I’m in here several times a week. And I just bailed you out—”

“I know. On a felony assault charge.” She shot him her best steely-eyed look. “You wouldn’t dare.”

He stared back. Neither of them blinked. “Want

to try me?" His voice was soft, which carried far more impact than if he'd shouted it.

She knew what he meant and how he meant it. It was her imagination that put an erotic twist on his words, made it an invitation to something far more. Her pulse fluttered and for a second she stood there, mesmerized by the curve of his mouth. Heat crawled up her face. She blinked. "No."

"I'm glad we got that settled." He held out the jacket and cap. "You want to go home. I want to take you home. What's the problem?"

She took them, taking care not to touch her fingers to his in the process. "The problem is..." What? She was going to tell him she was pissed her sister had dumped bailing her out on the enemy? No way. She was going to confess that even when he was being a macho bonehead, he turned her on? Hardly. She settled for the third truth, leaving the first two out. "I don't like for someone to tell me what to do."

"This is the deal, honey—"

"The name's Sunny, not Honey."

"It's a natural law. In every situation in life, someone has to be in charge. If it's a situation I'm a part of, then I'm the one in charge."

Could he possibly be any more arrogant? But she was worn out and she just wanted to be home.

Turning down a ride from him felt a little like cutting off her nose to spite her face. Principled didn't have to mean stupid. She'd lost it with Meeks today and she wasn't too far from losing it again. She was skating on the edge. Probably best to skip the reporters out front. Her temper and her mouth might get her into even more trouble. She shrugged into the jacket and crammed the cap down on her head.

"Fine. Take me home."

"Are you always so gracious?"

"Are you always so gallant?"

He looked as if we wanted to deliver a smart-ass comeback. Instead he started walking and she had to hurry to keep up. "I'm parked close to the door. It's the yellow Corvette."

Figured. A sexy muscle car. Her automobile weakness. Precisely the car at the top of her "hot" list. Everything about the man screamed testosterone.

Ten minutes. Fifteen at tops. Surely she could put up with him that long.

5

"WAS IT ON THE NEWS?" she asked, a marked weariness in her tone.

Cade made a right out of the parking lot, avoiding the news vans in front of the building. "The five o'clock."

He caught her nod out of the corner of his eye. Quiet descended on the car as he navigated downtown Memphis.

He'd never met such a—she defied description—woman in his life as Sunny Templeton. Alternately aggravating, amusing, appealing, the woman had actually shooed him like he was a pesky dog. But there was an energy about her, a presence, almost…and even though he didn't go in for this kind of crap…a connection. Even now, he sensed exhaustion rolling off her in waves, lapping at him.

He drove past the Christmas decorations mounted on the light posts. He hadn't lied when he told her she wasn't his type. She was intense and he didn't do intense women. However, the implication she didn't appeal to him was, unfortunately, a lie. When he'd grabbed her arm, a surge of want had rocked through him at the touch of her skin beneath his fingertips despite the fact that she looked tired and waterlogged, and that her hair alternately stuck out at odd angles or lay flat against her head. She was having what his sister termed "a bad hair day."

He glanced at her from the corner of his eye. Her face was more interesting than pretty, her purple eyes even more arresting in person. High cheekbones. A strong nose. Her mouth was a shade too wide. There was nothing delicate or cute about her but her face's angular sensuality drew him. And she had a nice ass, too. Hey, he was a man. Like he wasn't supposed to notice.

He'd deliberately played the Marlene card. He was sure blaming Marlene got him further than the truth. He'd been *compelled* to shield her from media circling on the front sidewalk. There was something about her that called to him, summoned him on an elemental level. He'd felt it when he saw that flyer but it was all the stronger when he met her. And wouldn't she think he was crazy as hell if he told her that?

If push had come to shove, he would've tossed her over his shoulder and hauled her out of there. Whatever it took to protect her, even if he was shielding her from her own stubbornness.

And he needed to clear up the Meeks issue. This was probably his one chance. Other than passing along whatever Jones uncovered on Meeks, if and when he had information, there was no reason for their paths to cross again. "Those ads we did with Meeks—" she turned and looked at him "—weren't politically motivated. Our business was feeling the crunch of a new competitor's ad campaign. We needed the exposure so we hooked up with him."

She laughed abruptly, startling him. "I'd have preferred to think you at least believed in him."

"Yeah, me too."

So much for that. He slowed down about a block from her house, watching for the turn.

"How'd you know where I live anyway? I just thought about it, I never gave you the address." Her voice held a slight huskiness that tightened his gut. She pulled off the ball cap and ran her fingers through her hair. It was shorter than it had been in the flyer. He liked it better this way.

"Your address was on the paperwork your sister

filled out. And don't forget, it's my job to find people that don't want to be found."

It should be the next right. He put on his blinker.

"Just drop me at the corner," she said.

"I don't think so. I'll see you to the door." There was no way in hell he was dropping her at the corner. Her neighborhood was an older section, on the fringes of revitalization but not quite there yet. Most of the aged row houses bore bars on the lower floor windows. It wasn't exactly the safest section of the city.

"You know—" she said, her annoyance evident.

He made a split-second decision to go straight rather than turn.

"Hey!" She cut herself off and looked over her shoulder. "You missed it. That was it."

"Yeah. You were so busy complaining *you* missed the paparazzi camped in front of your house." He assumed it was her house. It was unlikely they were hounding anyone else in this neighborhood. "Does this run behind your place?" He turned into the narrow alley without waiting on her answer.

It had a griminess universal to alleyways. Garbage littered the edge of the graffiti-covered back wall. A rusted washing machine listed drunkenly to one side amidst an assortment of plastic kids' toys missing various parts, like a Big Wheel, minus the wheel.

He stopped and let the car idle. "Which one is yours?"

She shook her head. "I'm not getting out back here. Drop me off up front. I'll deal with them."

An idea struck him, although she didn't seem the type, but sometimes you never knew. "Do you like all the coverage? Being in the limelight?"

She shot him a squelching look. "Don't be ridiculous. This past month has been a nightmare."

"Then it's crazy to go through them when you can go in this way."

"There are rats back here and I'm not getting out with rats."

As if on cue, his headlights pinpointed a rat the size of a small house cat at the corner of one of the garages that ran along the back of the row houses.

Sunny clenched her hands together. "See? They're awful. I never park in the garage because of them. I never even open my back door going into the garage." She shook her head. "I'm not getting out back here." Resolution underscored her words.

Cade considered himself a reasonably intelligent man. He had quite a bit of experience with the fairer sex and he also dealt with Marlene and his sister, Gracie, on a regular basis, which was a veritable trial by fire…and come to think of it, Sunny sort of reminded him a little of both Gracie and Marlene—just this side short of a force of nature. He could rant and rave, he could attempt to persuade, but he knew this woman wasn't getting out of his car back here. But he hadn't outwitted the news and the paparazzi this long to let them win now.

When plan A failed, a good bond-enforcement agent proceeded to plan B, and if there was no plan B, he improvised.

"I'll pull into your garage and walk you to your door. I'll make sure you get inside rat-free."

She shook her head again, looking so wretched, vulnerable, and determined it sort of tugged on his heartstrings, which he could've sworn had disappeared a long time ago. "I can't. If one of those things brushed against me or ran across my foot… I know you think I'm a pain in the ass. *I* think I'm a pain in the ass, but I cannot get out of this car back here."

A nice guy would deny she was a pain in the ass, but he wasn't and she was. "Okay. I'll unlock the door, come back to the car and carry you inside, thereby eliminating any remote possibility of contact with a rat."

Consternation chased across her face in the shadowed interior. "You can't do that. I weigh too much."

Cade silently counted to five for patience. First he was a pervert, then a pest, now a weakling. "I bench-press more than three hundred pounds on a regular basis. Since I'm pretty damn sure you weigh less than that, we're okay."

She made a funny, quirky face.

"I'm not worried about you. I don't want to be dropped."

He bit back an oath. "I'm stronger than I obviously look." Why didn't she just lop his nuts off and hand them to him? "Look, I just want to get you safely inside so I can go home and have a nice dinner." His instinct had shouted that she'd be trouble. Unfortunately that same instinct demanded he protect her.

"Girlfriend waiting?"

"No. My stomach's waiting. To be fed. Can we just get on with this?"

"I must've missed something. I didn't ask you to bring me home. You insisted. No, that's not true. You pulled a caveman stunt and threatened to carry me out if I didn't go willingly. I guess I'm lucky you were at least going to carry me outside rather than dragging me by my hair."

"I thought about it," he drawled, "but you need longer hair if I'm going to get a really good dragging grip."

She narrowed her eyes and he had the distinct impression she wanted to plant her hands on her hips but there wasn't room in the car. "I asked to be dropped out front but no. So, let's get it straight, *honey, I*'m not the one being difficult."

"That's a matter of opinion since you're the one refusing to let me get you safely inside through the back door." She'd nailed one thing straight on. She was a pain in his ass.

She threw up her hands. "Okay, okay. Fine. Be a macho he-man knight riding in to the rescue in a yellow Corvette. Whatever. I'm hungry, too. In fact I'll settle for a mediocre dinner." Her stomach growled, punctuating her remark.

Macho he-man knight riding in to the rescue in a yellow Corvette. A definite step up from a caveman. He bit back a triumphant smile at having finally worn her down and being that much closer to delivering her home safely. "Which one is yours?"

"Third one." She dug in her purse and pulled out a set of keys. "Here's the garage key," she said, handing it over.

Her fingers brushed his and a funny little zing shot through him.

Cade jumped out of the car and unlocked the garage door. The wind howled through the alley, slicing through his jacket. He raised the door and loped back to the car. He pulled into the parking spot and killed the engine but left the lights on. He had no desire to stumble around in the dark. Rats weren't his favorite, either. He held the ring with its key assortment out to her. "Back door key?"

Silently she handed it back to him. He got out and pulled down the garage door before unlocking the back door and returning to the car.

The garage smelled musty and dank as if it hadn't seen sunlight or fresh air in a long time. Most people crammed their garage full of junk. Hers stood totally empty except for his car. She obviously didn't use the garage for anything.

Sunny opened the car door and took off her seat belt. "I feel ridiculous," she said, "so let's just get this done as soon as possible."

"You sure? I was hoping we could drag it out for a while."

She ignored his sarcasm and sat as if waiting for the guillotine. "Okay. I'm ready."

Her marked lack of enthusiasm wasn't exactly flattering.

He bent down. "Put your arms around my neck." She looped her hands together behind his head and suddenly her cheek was very, very close to his mouth and her scent, fresh and clean and womanly despite her jail stint, chased away the garage's dankness.

"Like this?" she said with a slight hitch, her breath warm against his jaw.

"Like that." He slid one arm beneath her knees, the other behind her shoulder and lifted her out of the car. He straightened. Her right breast pressed against his chest and her hip snugged low against his belly while her scent teased around him.

His heart thudded inside his chest and his body tightened. It was like striking a match to a gas flame. Her arms tightened around his neck and her eyes widened as if she also felt the explosion of heat between them.

Her fingers curled against his neck and her lips parted. Instinctively he dipped his head. Her breath mingled with his….

They both jerked away simultaneously.

"The door's that way—" Her breath gusted against his neck.

"Hold on—"

Just get her in the house. That was all he needed to do. He'd wanted her before he'd ever met her. And right now want was an ache inside him. But wanting her was…complicated, because he didn't exactly understand why he wanted her. And when it came to women, Cade didn't do complicated.

SUNNY REMINDED HERSELF to breathe. Breathing was good. Kissing Cade Stone—not so good. Actually, it'd probably be very good, but not so smart.

His heart thudded against her shoulder and she felt fluttery inside. She needed her head examined. Maybe she'd concussed herself earlier today and hadn't realized it. His arms were like bands of steel beneath her shoulders and knees. She drew a steadying breath, inhaling the heady scent of man and leather.

He shouldered open her back door and carried her into the kitchen, shouldering it closed once again. She released her hold on his neck and he promptly deposited her onto her own two feet, as if he was as eager to release her as she was to be released. She stepped back from him, coming up against the door.

What had just happened? Well, she knew what had almost happened. She just didn't know why. And surely she wasn't disappointed that he hadn't kissed her? She couldn't possibly be frustrated with herself that she'd been a breath away from tossing caution to the wind and kissing him.

The air between them practically quivered with an elemental pull.

"I thought you said I wasn't your type," she

challenged, still slightly breathless from the sheer magnetism of his nearness.

He quirked one dark eyebrow. "You're not."

Thinner, younger, prettier all came to her mind. Somehow she didn't think he bothered too much with smart.

"Then why'd you almost kiss me?" She'd never been one to beat around the bush or play games. She shifted closer, drawn to him, as if bound to him by an invisible cord.

He closed the gap between them and her heart pounded. "You know, I thought *you* almost kissed me and you claimed *I* wasn't *your* type."

"You're definitely not. At all. No way. In fact, I knew if I met you I wouldn't like you and I don't." Well, there was like and then there was *like.* Lust, which seemed to be alive and well where he was concerned, was an altogether different matter.

He lowered his head, his jaw nearly brushing her own. Anticipation shivered down her spine at his almost-touch. "Funny," he said, the low gravel of his voice stroking along her nerve endings, "I'm pretty sure I don't like you either."

She stood on tiptoe, her lips nearly touching his ear and whispered the burning question. "Then why'd you want to kiss me?"

"Damned if I know." He cupped her chin in his

big hand and tilted her face up to his. His tawny eyes appeared smoky in the near-dark. "All you've done is insult me since I've met you." He brushed his thumb against the corner of her lower lip and her knees threatened to give way. "You know, you're a very frustrating woman."

She braced her hands on his shoulders, his muscle rock hard beneath the supple leather. "I'm frustrating?" She nipped the tip of his thumb. "Have you looked in a mirror lately? I didn't threaten to carry you out of the police station slung over my shoulder."

"Only because you knew you couldn't. Otherwise, I'm sure you would have." He smiled that lopsided smile and she knew that none of her fantasies about Cade Stone had prepared her for this. "You were being noncooperative. You didn't leave me any choice." His tawny eyes pierced her like a laser. "I'm more interested in why you *didn't* kiss me than why you almost did."

Good Lord, he had the most sensuous mouth. Had she ever so desperately wanted just a kiss?

"It struck me as a very bad choice. I decided kissing you would be more trouble than it was worth."

"Who knew?" His head blocked the light, enclosing them in intimate shadow, his lips brushing hers even as he spoke. "We have something in common because I thought the same thing."

And then his mouth was on hers and Sunny realized that while she'd definitely been kissed before, she'd never *really* been kissed.

6

"I SHOULD LEAVE," Cade said. Dammit, he'd *known* kissing her was a bad idea. Just like he'd known meeting her was a bad idea. And staying any longer sure as hell was a bad idea. He'd done what he came to do. "Do you need anything before I go?"

Sunny's cell phone rang, interrupting what he was sure was going to be a *no.* She fished it out of the purse still slung over her shoulder. She looked at the flashing display with a perplexed frown, apparently not recognizing the number, and answered the call. "Hello?"

He didn't mean to eavesdrop, but it was damn near impossible not to hear the woman's strident voice on the other end when he was still standing right in front of Sunny. "Sunny, this is Tosha Mackey with WMPH news. We'd like to tell your side of the story. What do you think of City Councilman Meeks's assertion that you tried to kill him today?"

"No comment."

Sunny disconnected the call. Before she could draw a breath it rang again. She gave it another go. A man's voice rushed. "Do you regret what—"

She hung up on the caller and pushed the cell phone's off button. She drew a deep breath and a terse smile played around her lips. "Yes, there is one more thing you can do for me."

Despite sounding calm, despite the smile, she radiated fury.

"What is it?"

"What is the absolute worst dive bar you know?"

"The Three-Star," he answered automatically. The Three-Star Bar a couple of blocks off of Beale generated plenty of business for AA Atco. Drunken brawls were a daily occurrence, not to mention the occasional prostitution bust and drug deal. "Why?"

"Can you drop me off there?" She thought he'd *drop her off* at The Three-Star Bar? Maybe when hell froze over. "If it's out of your way I can call a cab."

"Exactly why do you want to go to the Three-Star? I missed that part."

She sidestepped around him. "I have been hounded, harassed and been made a laughingstock for the past month. It was so bad at one point that I didn't leave my house for two weeks. Today I made a mistake but to tell you the truth, I don't regret it." She paced while she talked, back and forth across the small kitchen. "I'm not sorry in the least that I rammed into that slimy little toad."

He barely stopped himself from clamping his hand over her mouth. If she said that to the wrong person she didn't have a hope in hell of not doing jail time. "You might want to keep that tidbit private."

She stopped in her tracks. "Private! Private? Nothing in my life has been private for the past month. I thought my cell phone number was private, but apparently not any longer."

He was looking at a woman who'd been pushed past her limits. She was one step beyond reason.

She resumed pacing. "I'm not playing the game any longer. I'm not going to sit huddled in this house with no food and no phone and worry myself sick over whether I'm going to jail for a felony and how I'm going to pay the fines and what it'll do to my business if I wind up in the slammer and what it'll be like if I get a cell mate like Spanky." Who the hell was Spanky? "Nope." She planted herself in front of him, arms crossed over her chest, her chin tilted aggressively. "I'm going to the Three-Star and getting knee-crawling drunk." He'd wager she'd never been knee-crawling drunk in her life. It would've made the news during the past month or at some point in her campaign, plus he'd read enough about her that he had a pretty good idea of the fundamental Sunny Templeton. On a sane, rational day she wasn't the let's-get-drunk type, knee-crawling or otherwise. Sane and rational, however, seemed to have momentarily vacated her premises. "If they want a story, I'll give them a story."

"That would be a mistake," he said in a neutral tone.

"It wouldn't be the first one I've made. Don't worry about it. I'll call a cab. Or my friend Joanie." She started to turn on her cell phone.

He stayed her with his hand on hers, thinking quick on his feet. She would definitely regret this if she went through with it. And given her mood, if she kissed some guy after a few drinks the same way she'd just kissed him, Cade would have to rip the guy's head off. He had no right at all to feel territorial but he wanted to snarl at just the idea. Altogether a bad situation for everyone involved. Her friend Joanie would probably talk some sense into her. Or maybe not. He wasn't willing to take that chance.

There was only one way to make sure she didn't get within spitting distance of the Three-Star or any other bar. "No need to call a cab or Joanie. I'll give you a ride."

"You're sure?"

He didn't know if situational hysteria was an actual term. If it wasn't, it should be. That's what he'd call this. He considered slapping her to see if she'd snap out of it but he wasn't sure he could actually hit a woman, and if she didn't snap out of it, she'd probably slap him back…and wind up calling her friend.

"No problem. I can even wait if you want to shower first and change clothes." A little time and a hot shower might calm her down, change her mind.

"Oh, no. I'm ready to go now."

Not that he needed additional proof that she was over the edge, but no woman in her right mind would go out with her hair doing that crazy sticking out thing and her mascara smeared under her eyes, even if was only heading to the Three-Star. He actually found her very sexy despite the hair and makeup and she'd definitely outclass any other woman at the Three-Star but still….

"Okay." Mindful of her rat phobia, he scooped her up in his arms, thinking it was downright disconcerting how right she felt there, and opened the back door. "Then we'll go now."

Damn, she was going to be mad. Eventually she'd thank him for saving her from herself.

Well, maybe.

"SON OF A BITCH," Cade swore softly under his breath.

"What?" Sunny said.

Apparently not softly enough.

"No problem. I missed my turn."

He had fully planned to turn Sunny over to Marlene. It would've been the perfect win-win situation. Marlene truly seemed to be an advocate for Sunny. With a big house and a calm, soothing nature, she would've managed to keep Sunny safe and sound at her house until the Three-Star urge had passed. Sunny could enjoy a hot shower, a good meal and a sound night's sleep without worrying about someone trying to snap her picture or land an interview.

He'd counted on Marlene being through with dinner and home. He hadn't, however, counted on Martin being there, too. From the looks of things, they'd decided on more than raw fish and rice.

Martin's truck sat in the drive next to Marlene's car. The redbrick Colonial stood dark, even the Christmas tree in the front window wasn't turned on. Not quite eight o'clock. Cade didn't figure Marlene was teaching Martin to knit in the dark.

"This can't be the way to the bar." Accusation

sparked in her eyes. "Dive bars aren't usually in upscale neighborhoods."

This whole operation was going from bad to worse. There'd been no way in hell he could let her walk out of the front of that jail and climb into a cab and then he'd been equally unable to turn her loose at *any* bar in her present state of mind, much less the Three-Star.

"No. It's not the way to the bar. You're not going to the bar. The bar is a bad decision." He jerked his thumb over his shoulder at the dark house. "That was Marlene's house. I thought you could stay with her. That was a good decision. Unfortunately, she seems to be entertaining this evening."

And now Martin was screwing Marlene—not his worst nightmare but he damn sure wasn't happy about it because it could very well mess things up at the office just when they were getting back on their feet. Not to mention it totally shot to hell his plan to let Marlene smother Sunny in goodwill. He could hardly knock on the door and drop her off now. And if Martin broke Marlene's heart, or even dinted it, Cade was gonna kick Martin's ass up one side of Poplar Street and back down the other, father or not.

"You lied."

She could add it to his ongoing list of sins. "I did."

"I want to go to that bar."

"Nope. I can't let you do that."

She drummed her fingers on the armrest. "We covered this earlier. You don't *let* me do anything. If you won't drop me off at the Three-Star, take me back home."

That definitely wasn't what she needed with photographers hanging around out front. "Uh-uh."

"Drop me off at a friend's."

Not a chance. There was no guarantee her friend would squash Sunny's plan. "I don't think so."

"I don't need a keeper. Especially not you."

"For the record, I followed your campaign. You strike me as a very smart, very responsible woman who makes sound decisions most of the time. This isn't one of those times. Pardon me for pointing it out, honey. But you haven't done such a stellar job of keeping yourself out of trouble today."

"You can't just throw me in your car—"

"I didn't throw."

"—*put* me in your car and take me somewhere I don't want to go. That's kidnapping." Outrage sent her voice an octave higher.

He shrugged. Technically she had a point. He trusted she'd see it differently later. "Just think of it as protective custody."

"You're not going to handcuff me, are you?"

"Only if you want me to."

"Your caveman tactics are really getting on my nerves."

"I hate that for you."

"You can at least tell me where we're going."

He'd known she was going to be a pain in his ass but there was no getting around it.

"We're going to the one place I know you won't get yourself into any more trouble. My house."

SHE WASN'T SURE WHETHER she wanted to laugh or cry. Or maybe scream. Screaming might relieve some of the frustration she felt but it would probably startle him while he was driving and that would be a bad thing because then they might wreck and even if they weren't both killed or maimed that would make her responsible for two accidents in one day and it would be a crying shame to be responsible for wrecking such a beautiful car. So no crying, no lunatic laughing and no screaming.

Instead she rubbed her right thumb over her hummingbird ring, grounding herself. Hummingbirds bypassed tough and bitter exteriors to find the hidden treasures, the nectar beneath. *Chill, Sunny, and think.*

Okay, so maybe showing up at a dive bar and getting smashed and trashed *wasn't* the best idea.

At the time it felt like she was *doing* something, taking control.

She firmly believed that nothing in life was incidental. People came to you, crossed your path for a reason. You either had a lesson to learn from them or you were meant to teach them something. Perhaps both.

Where was the lesson in Cade Stone? She couldn't say she liked him, but she'd been drawn to him from the moment she'd seen that billboard.

Protective custody. The realization crept in on quiet cat feet—she felt safe. His infuriating tactics might rile her and cause all kinds of hormonal havoc, and he obviously considered her an equal annoyance, but for the time being, for as long as he had her in protective custody, she was safe. He'd stand between her and the paparazzi, her and Meeks, her and whomever. He'd keep her safe but there was nothing safe about him.

"You asleep?"

"No. I'm having a Zen moment."

"What?"

"I'm trying to think."

"There's a barbecue joint up here. I'm going through the drive-thru. You need something to eat. What do you want?"

Okay, it was safety with a rough edge, not

warm, cuddly safe. Did he have to be so high-handed about everything? "What if I don't like barbecue?"

He slowed down and made a right into the parking lot of what was little more than a shack. A weathered wooden pig silhouette, minus one leg, was mounted on the top with The Best Barbecue written across the pig in faded paint.

"Do you like barbecue?"

"Well, yeah. But what if I didn't?"

He pulled up to the order window. "Then I guess you'd tell me, wouldn't you? What do you want?"

"There's no menu sign. What do they have?"

"Pork."

"What else?"

He grinned and Sunny was glad she was sitting, because she wasn't too sure she'd have still been standing, otherwise. "You can get it on a bun or without a bun."

Sunny laughed. Do tell. The caveman actually possessed a sense of humor. "Then I think I'll have the pork. On the bun. Fries?"

"Jerline can fix you up with some fries." He rolled down his window. A big woman, Sunny'd guess in her mid-fifties, with red frizzy hair, a yellow mumu and rhinestone-rimmed cat-eye sunglasses opened the glass for the order window. Jerline was *colorful.*

"What's up, Big Daddy?" Jerline sounded as if she'd smoked about a gazillion packs of unfiltered Camels from the time she was born. "How's my favorite hunk tonight?"

"Ready to get home and let the tired fall off. How're you?"

"My arthritis has been acting up in my left knee but I'm ready to go dancin' whenever you are. What can I get you tonight?"

"Three sandwiches, two fries."

"Coleslaw?" Sunny asked.

"And a coleslaw," he tacked on to the order.

"Uh-huh. Who's that with ya? You steppin' out on me?"

"Nah, I just found her by the road. You know you're the only one for me."

"You smooth-tongued devil." She looked over her shoulder and yelled, "Clarence, I need three little gos, two fry and a slaw. It's Cade. Put on extra meat." She looked back to Cade. "We'll fix you up. Gracie called and we're all set to cater the Christmas party. Sure appreciate the business."

Sunny guessed they'd have pork at their Christmas party.

"Good deal. It wouldn't be the Christmas party without The Best Barbecue." Sunny tried not to stare but he had a nice profile, strong, commanding.

Jerline leaned her elbow on the windowsill. "She said Linc's getting hitched."

"Yep."

"To some wedding planner gal."

"Uh-huh."

"You know what that means don'tcha?"

"That Linc's lost his mind?" His dry quip didn't strike Sunny as altogether joking. It didn't leave much ambiguity as to how he felt about the matter. Was it marriage in general or just his brother in particular? And was it any of her business? No.

"Get out." Jerline swatted toward the open window and giggled in a gravelly baritone. "It means you're next."

"Haven't you heard?" Cade said. "I'm already married." Sunny's breath locked in her throat. He couldn't have kissed her like that if he was married. Well, he could, but dammit.... "To my job."

She had no idea what Jerline said. He wasn't married! Close on the heels of breathing again came the realization that it shouldn't—make that *didn't*—matter a whit to her whether he was married or a free agent.

Jerline handed a big brown paper sack out the window. "There you go. Bon appetit." Cade passed it to Sunny. "And don't do nuthin I wouldn't." She waved. "Nice to meet ya, hon."

Sunny put the bag in her lap. "Nice to meet you, too," Sunny said, although the meeting had been totally nonparticipative on her part.

"Sounds like a nice girl." Jerline grinned, revealing teeth so startlingly white and straight they had to be dentures. "Mark my words, you're next, Big Daddy."

"Later."

"Uh-huh."

He exited through the drive-thru.

"Big Daddy? You picked me up on the side of the road?"

"Jerline calls all the men Big Daddy, and the other, it was just a joke."

"She's quite a character."

"You don't know the half." He shook his head. "Jerline's legally blind. It's a degenerative thing. She and Clarence have had some hard times."

Sunny had an aha moment. "That's why she said I *sounded* like a nice girl."

He nodded. "Go ahead and eat if you want to."

"No. I'd rather shower first." Good lord, it felt unbearably intimate to talk about showering in the close confines of his car when she knew she'd be in *his* shower.

"I understand."

"I, uh—" This felt awkward. She didn't exactly

owe him an apology. It was more of an acknowledgment that her judgment had been just a little skewed earlier. “I guess going to a bar wasn’t exactly a good idea.”

He pulled up to a stop sign and glanced over at her. “No. Not exactly.”

At that moment, with moonlight slanting through the window, etching his face in partial shadow and light, recognition slammed her. She swallowed a gasp. The eyes, the tilt of the head, the nose and chin. She’d started it after the billboards had gone up. It must have been instinct on her part, subconscious inspiration. Her stained-glass project.

Cade Stone was the wolf.

Her wolf.

7

"YOU'LL NEED TO DO SOMETHING about your car tomorrow," Cade said, breaking the silence that had stretched between them. She'd kind of looked at him funny back at the stop sign and then clammed up. He found a silent Sunny disquieting. Who the hell knew what she was cooking up over there? At least when she was talking he knew what trouble she was headed for.

"Thanks. I know. It'll have to be towed to a body shop. That is, if the insurance company doesn't total it out. My poor baby. It's a '67 Mustang ragtop." Her voice rang with the pride of a true muscle car lover.

No kidding? "Sweet. How'd you wind up with that?"

"I saw it by the side of the road with a For Sale sign and I knew I had to have it."

"Just like that?"

"Just like that. Love at first sight."

"Are you always so impulsive?"

"Only with the important things. When I see something I want. I wasn't even looking for a car but I saw it and that was it. Sometimes things, people just call to you whether you want them to or not." Gooseflesh prickled over him. That was exactly the way it'd been when he'd seen her flyer. She'd called to him. And no, he hadn't wanted her to. "I made sure it was in good running shape before I bought it. I'm not a total nitwit." He didn't remember saying she was. "This is a nice car."

She ran a reverent hand over the dash, lightly stroking a finger over the chrome cluster gauges mounted above the hand brake and gearshift. It was a very sensual, very sexy move…at least to a man who was into cars. Cade swallowed. Hard. In a heartbeat the atmosphere thickened, awareness arcing between them. She trailed her finger along the edge of the leather seat. "Nice leather. Very supple."

He remembered the sweep of her fingers against his neck earlier, the feel of her skin against his. "Thanks."

He downshifted to turn and his arm brushed hers. Even through both their jackets it reverberated through him. Was that a soft gasp from her? "Sorry."

"No problem."

He gripped the wheel tighter. He wanted her to

touch him the way she'd touched the car. He wanted her to slip her hand between his knees, trail her fingers up his thigh, stroke his—

"'72?"

"What?"

"Is it a '72?"

Oh. The year of the car. Right. "Close. '73." Keep her talking. Then he couldn't lapse into some sexual fantasy about her and him in the damn car. "Is your Mustang a manual or automatic? Six or eight cylinder?"

"It's a 390 V-8," she said, the slight huskiness in her voice firing through him. "Manual. Shifting's half the fun of driving."

Oh, sweet— He could practically feel her hand wrapped around him, shifting him higher and higher.

His mailbox came into view.

"We're almost there," Cade said.

He'd never been so damn glad to see his driveway in his life.

THANK GOODNESS. Another few minutes of talking cars and she'd be in serious trouble. Forget it, she was already in serious trouble. He smelled of aftershave, leather and man in the cocooned intimacy of the car. She'd seen the heat in his eyes, the tightening of his grip on the steering wheel. She wasn't the only one feeling the heat. She was hot, flushed, achy. She wanted the same thing she'd wanted since the first time she'd seen him: she wanted to feel him inside her, know the taste of his mouth, the touch of his skin, his scent mingling with her own. But now she wanted it with an intensity she'd never known before.

She wet her lips with the tip of her tongue. She desperately needed some distance. Cade put on his blinker to make a left turn into a driveway just past a high-end subdivision, but wasn't part of it. "Here we are." He waited on a car coming from the other direction.

She jumped at the chance to focus on something other than a need for this man that dampened her thighs and left her breasts feeling full, ripe. A stone wall farther down the road indicated another high-dollar development. "It looks as if subdivisions have sprung up all around you."

He quirked a brief smile. "Yeah, just me sitting in the middle of my twenty acres."

"You could make a fortune selling to a developer."

"That's never going to happen. This land has been in my family for over a hundred and fifty years."

Sunny had to grudgingly give him points on that. Most people would take the money and run. There was nothing wrong with selling to developers, but it said something about him that preserving his heritage was outside a price tag.

Between the headlights and the moon she had a good view of the property. Tall sprawling trees flanked a long paved driveway. It led to a saltbox style house with a front stoop. The drive bisected around to a barn that sported a vintage metal sign over the double doors to the left and then straight ahead to what had to be the back door. "It's beautiful."

"It's not fancy."

"It doesn't have to be." The stained-glass artist inside her found the clean lines of the house and barn aesthetically pleasing.

He stopped the car at the edge where the driveway met the walkway.

"I'll get you inside and then I'll park the car. No one actually farms the land anymore so I converted the barn into a garage."

Sunny opened the door. Cold air rushed inside. Before she knew it he was there, his hand on her arm, helping her out of the low-slung sports car. It was an old-fashioned, gallant gesture that left her all fluttery inside. A patchwork of irregular stones interspersed with grass formed the walk.

Cade unlocked and opened the door, flipped on

a light and ushered her inside. Sunny stopped in the foyer and absorbed the feel, the smell of the house.

She liked old houses but, like people, they all had different personalities. Her parents had thought she was nutty as a fruitcake when she'd mentioned it as a child. Nadine teased her that she was the house whisperer.

Mrs. Pearl, however, had understood. Sunny *felt* the energy every time she "met" a house. This one was nice. It felt like a haven, warm and welcoming. She sensed its embrace, but it was also lonely. She felt its desire for a family to fill its space once again, to have children's laughter echo off its walls, to know the joy and contentment of lives intertwined. It spoke to her as her own house never had.

"Nice house."

"Thank you." He was pleased. She knew it as clearly as she knew this had been a place of joy in times past.

Stairs led upwards, to the left of the door. Wood planks formed the flooring, tongue-in-groove wood the ceiling. "I love all the wood, especially the ceiling."

"My great-great-grandfather cut the timber on the property, hauled it by mule and wagon to a mill outside of Memphis. He used it to build the house."

A den lay to the right. What would've been a

parlor to the left. "This is original wood? That's fantastic!" She ran a hand over the worn banister that had known a hundred and fifty years of touches.

"All of the interior wood's original. Most of the exterior's been replaced." He put the bag of takeout on a small table in the foyer and gestured for her to mount the stairs. "The bedrooms and the bath are up here."

She preceded him up the stairs, aware of him behind her, his body heat, his energy pulsing around her with each step she climbed. She paused at the landing at the top, unsure where to go next. He stopped behind her, his breath stirring against her hair. He indicated a door to the right, halfway down the short hallway. "That's my room. Take a right."

She stepped aside and let him take the lead. He bypassed the first door in favor of the one farthest from his. He switched on a bedside lamp. "Here you go. The bathroom's at the end of the hallway. There's only one. I'll get you sheets for the bed and a towel and washcloth."

She nodded absently, looking around, taking in the room. Cream-colored walls, a white counterpane on a pencil-post bed, white cut-lace curtains at the window, an arts and crafts nightstand, an antique chifforobe and a cream upholstered chair filled the room. A multicolored rag rug and a watercolor of a wildflower field in bloom lent the room a burst of color. A pool of light spilled over the bed and part of the floor from the bedside lamp.

After the day—make that the month—she'd had, it settled about her like a balm to her soul. She suddenly knew without a doubt that coming with Cade Stone was exactly what she'd needed, as crazy and irrational as it had sounded. She needed a brief hiatus from her world.

Sunny turned to face Cade. He stood, arms crossed, his tawny eyes watching, his chiseled features inscrutable.

"This is a wonderful room," she said, breaking the quiet, her breath catching in her throat at his nearness. What was it about this man that affected her so?

"Glad you like it." He didn't smile but she saw a glimmer of approval in his eyes. "You wanted a shower first, right?"

"Dinner would taste a lot better if I was clean." She hadn't been ill-treated at the jail, but it had smelled of sweat and God knew what else. She shuddered. "I literally need to wash the day off."

Cade nodded. "I've never been arrested, but just taking in skips I shower twice a day."

Him in the shower. There was a thought. A dangerous thought considering she was in his house, in a bedroom. With him. Bed conveniently located right behind them. The memory of his hands tangled in her hair, his mouth devouring hers, his tongue mating with her own fed her imagination. Her pulse shifted into high gear and she tried very hard to push aside the mental image of him naked, wreathed in steam, hot water sluicing over his broad shoulders and chest, streaming down the flat plane of his belly, his jutting erection.... Enough!

But the damage to her equilibrium was done. He seemed to fill the bedroom, his scent drawing her. Like a movie that refused to be paused, she saw the two of them together in the shower, his big hands with those lean fingers soaped and tracing lather over every inch of her, paying special attention to her arousal-slicked feminine folds, her breasts, the curves of her hips, her buttocks. She wasn't sure if she *liked* him, but there wasn't a bit of doubt that she *wanted* him.

His eyes darkened and his gaze swept her lips and they tingled as if he'd traced them with his finger. The air nearly crackled with the tension between them.

Cade turned abruptly on his heel. "I've got to put the car away. I'll leave the sheets and towels outside your door. Come down when you're ready to eat."

Three strides carried him to the hall. He closed the door behind him, leaving her alone.

There were several moments of silence, then

Cade's measured tread approached her bedroom door and Sunny's pulse accelerated to warp speed. There was a pause and then his retreating footsteps.

"Wait," she called out. She crossed the room and opened the door. He stood poised at the top of the stairs, his tawny eyes watchful, leashed strength in the sculpted lines of his body.

A sudden case of nerves shifted her from one foot to the other. She pushed her hand through her hair. "I don't have, um, any clothes to change into. Do you happen to have any women's clothes here?" Part of her hoped fervently that he did. A green-eyed portion of her hoped not.

He nodded his head, "Yeah." Figured. "My sister has some stuff here—" he eyed her from head to toe, lingering at the pertinent parts in between, leaving her horribly self-conscious but enflamed nonetheless "—but you're a lot bigger than she is." Oh, great.

"Thank you. It's nice to know I'm a Sasquatch."

He threw his head back and laughed and Sunny felt something indefinable tug inside her. He shook his head, smiling. "Everyone's a Sasquatch compared to Gracie. Linc and I are big like Martin—" she assumed Martin was his father "—but Gracie, she's tiny like Mom was." She caught a glimpse of a shadow in his eyes and then it was gone.

She could've sworn the house offered a sigh of sadness.

She really, really wanted to ask about his mother but a sense of overstepping bounds held her back. Instead she pursued the clothing issue. "Do you maybe have something an old girlfriend left behind? At this point, I'm not picky." She wrinkled her nose. "I can't bear the thought of putting these clothes back on with Shelby County Jail all over them."

"No girlfriend clothes." He ran a hand over his head. "Go in the bathroom and strip down. Throw your clothes out into the hall and I'll toss them into the washer for you."

"That's great except that leaves me sitting naked in the bathroom until they wash and dry."

A wicked, wolfish smile curled his lips and glinted in his eyes. "No need to stay in the bathroom."

"I…uh…"

He grinned. "I'm just kidding. I'll give you a T-shirt to put on." Another one of those assessing looks that hardened her nipples into tight pearls. "It'll be longer on you than some of the skirts you would've seen tonight at the Three-Star. Hold tight."

He disappeared into his bedroom, flipping on the light. She caught a glimpse of a rather Spartan room with dark gray linens edged in black. He returned and walked over to her carrying a gray T-shirt. Gray wasn't her best color, but beggars couldn't be choosers. He held it up to her, setting her heart racing at the feel of his hands against her shoulders, his broad chest at eye level. "Yep, it'll work."

"Thank you." She practically snatched the garment, willing him to step away, give her some distance, take his tantalizing scent and touch out of sensory range.

"The shirt'll work, but as for the rest, even my sweats are going to be way too big on you."

Something wild and slightly wicked and daring danced through her. He was, after all, responsible for her being here without even a pair of spare panties. She offered her sweetest smile. "Then until you finish my laundry, I guess I'll just have to go commando."

8

"WATCH YOUR STEP," Cade cautioned Sunny, his heart thumping faster at the sight of her standing in the kitchen doorway. "It's two steps down."

She paused at the top step and looked around the room, her violet eyes lighting up with interest. She looked far more relaxed after her shower. He, however, felt far from relaxed.

Her hair, still damp from the shower, framed her face in soft waves. She'd taken care of the smeared mascara raccoon eyes. She looked slightly rumpled and sexy as hell—as if she'd just pulled on his T-shirt after a round of making love. Desire thrummed through him like a steady summer rain. He itched to run his hands through her thick, soft hair, plunder the hot sweetness of her mouth....

He'd barely made it out of her bedroom earlier without tumbling her backward onto the mattress. Her eyes had reflected her willingness. Even with his eyes closed he could have felt the attraction arcing between them. But she needed a shower, food and a good night's rest a hell of a lot more than she needed sex.

Walking away hadn't been easy and he'd taken his own sweet time putting away the car after he'd grabbed her clothes and tossed them in the washer. It had been damn impossible to put them in to wash without seeing the black panties and black bra she'd worn beneath her jeans and sweater.

It was better not to hear the shower running and know she was naked upstairs in his house. Being in the same room with her and not having his belly knotted with lust should've been easier now that she was downstairs. It wasn't. Maybe because she was one lousy T-shirt away from being naked. Granted, his T-shirt hung halfway to her very shapely knees and he saw women on a daily basis showing more leg but damn it to hell, he knew with gut-clenching, ball-tightening certainty that she was, as she'd so thoughtfully pointed out, "going commando."

"What an absolutely awesome room," she said. "It's…incredible."

She'd liked the rest of the house. He'd known she'd love this room. Despite her enthusiasm she swayed slightly on her feet. He recognized exhaustion and hunger.

"Sit. Eat. I'll tell you about it over dinner." Yep,

boring the hell out of her with house info was a heck of a lot better than him standing around aroused because she was nearly naked. "What do you want to drink? Beer? Wine? Water? Milk?"

"Beer." She smiled, a mixture of rue and sheepishness. "But I'll forego the knee-crawling drunk part."

Cade shrugged. "If you need to get knee-crawling drunk, here is a much better choice than the Three-Star. I promise I'll get you to bed safe."

Her eyes darkened and her tongue darted out to moisten her lower lip. "I'm not sure how safe you getting me to bed would be."

The getting her there wouldn't be a problem. Not climbing in with her, well, that was a different story. "I knew you were a smart woman." Don't talk about bed. Don't think about bed. Focus on food and drink. "Lager or ale?"

"Lager."

She settled on the worn leather bar seat while he pulled two bottles out of the fridge, snagged a couple of frozen mugs from the freezer and served them up. He'd set the take-out plates on the breakfast counter. Seemed sort of silly to sit at the table when it was just the two of them. He sat at the far end, leaving an empty stool between them, as much distance as possible.

She wrapped her fingers around the mug's frosted handle and took a long swallow. She made a low moan in the back of her throat. "Mmm. That's good. Just what I needed."

He'd be taking the mother of all cold showers if she ate and drank the entire meal with that level of enthusiasm. He'd seen women fondle a beer bottle with exaggerated suggestion or slowly, deliberately lick a spoon in a seductive way. He knew a deliberately seductive move when he saw it and Sunny's was totally spontaneous, which made it all the hotter because that was her instinctive response. She had his full attention, some parts more attentive than others.

He drank from his own mug. It was cold; maybe it'd cool him down.

She broke off a bite of barbecue sandwich. "So tell me about this room. I've never seen anything like it. I love it." She popped the bit into her mouth.

"It's my favorite part of the house. Has been since I was a kid." When he was young and they'd come for holidays or for an afternoon visit, this space had drawn him. It was one big room that ran the length of the rear of the house. From the hallway, the right half of the room held an enormous fireplace flanked by wooden rocking chairs. A long plank table with benches on either side sat in the middle of the room. To the left of the doorway was the kitchen and what he thought of as the greenhouse.

Christ, even the way she chewed her food turned him on—sort of slow, as if she was savoring every bite. She swallowed and broke another bite off the sandwich.

"So you grew up here?"

"No, the house has been passed down on my mother's side of the family. When I was a kid, my grandparents lived here. We lived on the other side of Memphis but this is where we had all the family get-togethers. Still do, in fact."

"How'd you come to live here?" She dragged a French fry through ketchup.

"My mother was an only child. She would've inherited the place. When Granny died, it went to me as the oldest grandson. I've always loved the place so I was happy to move out here and take care of it."

She gave him a sort of odd look. "So you protect it from encroaching development for future generations?"

He'd never really thought about it that way, he just did what he did instinctively. "I guess you could say that."

A smile played about her lips. "And this is your

favorite room? You spend a lot of time in here?" She seemed genuinely interested.

"Not as much time as when I was a kid. When the weather was too lousy to be outside this was our room of choice. My brother and I spent lots of rainy afternoons playing in our *fort.*" He grinned at the memory. "We'd drape one of Granny's quilts over the table, while Mom and Granny baked or canned fruit and vegetables or just sat by the fire and exchanged gossip. We were rowdy boys. One of us would piss the other one off, we'd fight and because I was the oldest and should have known better, I got sent to the parlor to cool my heels." Damn, he hadn't thought about that in years. He laughed. "It's still my least favorite room in the house."

She grinned and he felt a funny twinge inside. "I was always the one getting Nadine in trouble."

"Really? That's a shocker."

She wrinkled her nose at him and pointed to the left quarter of the room that was all glass, ceiling included. "When was that done? I'm assuming it wasn't when the house was built."

"No. The house was built in 1857. This was originally three rooms. The dining room with the fireplace was the kitchen. This part where the kitchen is now was a pantry and the greenhouse section was a child-birthing and sick room. If someone had a fever they couldn't afford for the whole household to catch it."

She nodded and pushed her hair behind one ear. A small diamond sparkled at the top of her lobe. "Makes sense."

"I'm sure things were changed some through the years, but there was a fire in 1958. Lightning struck that corner of the house. Luckily it was during a thunderstorm so the fire didn't do too much damage, but it was enough. My mother loved plants and had a green thumb. Grandpa, a farmer, had read about conservatories. He came up with this after the fire. It caused quite a stir. The neighbors thought Grandpa had lost it." He'd always loved the way his grandfather, a normally quiet man, would cackle when he recounted that story.

He caught himself. He didn't normally talk so much, especially not about his family, but Sunny's eyes hadn't glazed over yet. In fact, she seemed fascinated.

"That's a wonderful story. And did he have the pavers installed at the same time? You see it a lot now but not in the fifties."

His grandfather had laid six-by-six terra cotta pavers in the kitchen and glassed area. "Grandpa was a man before his time."

“She must’ve loved it. Do you keep the plants now?”

Potted herbs, a small lemon tree, ferns, an enormous pink Christmas cactus in full bloom and God and Gracie knew what else thrived. “Hardly. My sister inherited Mom’s green thumb. Another lager?” he asked, nodding toward her now-empty mug.

“I’m good. The barbecue was excellent, by the way.”

“Glad you liked it.” A smear of barbecue sauce clung to the corner of her lower lip. What would she do if he leaned over and licked it off? The trouble was once he licked that plump, ripe spot on her mouth, he’d want to lick other plump, ripe places. She hadn’t signed on for *come home with me so I can screw you blind.*

He pointed to the corner of her mouth. “You’ve got some barbecue sauce…”

She teased the tip of her tongue against the spot. “Better?”

“Yep.” No! Couldn’t the woman use a damn napkin? That wouldn’t send all the blood rushing to his cock. At least he didn’t think it would.

She shifted on the bar stool and her T-shirt slid off of one shoulder. A small tattoo gleamed on the back of her right shoulder.

“What’s the tat?”

"It's a hummingbird." She glanced over her shoulder with a smile. "Not your typical hummingbird design. It's a Native American interpretation."

"Right. I can see it now." A turquoise, red and black hummingbird hovered midflight against her shoulder's pale skin, its wings sweeping forward. He quelled the urge to reach out and trace it with his finger. "Why a hummingbird?"

"It's my totem." He must've looked perplexed. "You know, like a spirit guide. If I have a strong connection to someone, I can sense their totem."

"That's cool. It's a gift." Her deep-purple eyes widened in surprise. "My sister, Gracie, has touches of—" he didn't know what to call it "—not exactly clairvoyance but now and then she glimpses snapshots of the future."

He realized with a start that he'd divulged more to her in one dinner than he had to any of the women he'd ever dated for a four-week stint.

He stood abruptly. "Your clothes should be ready to go in the dryer."

"POINT ME IN THE RIGHT DIRECTION and I'll take care of it," Sunny said. Maybe if she hadn't realized his wolf connection earlier his abrupt shift now would've disconcerted her. But she knew exactly what had happened. She'd gotten too close, his guard was down and the moment he realized it he'd retreated. Men! And this one in particular.

Dinner had been…interesting. She'd loved hearing the house's history and about his family. It kept her mind off of Cecil and jail and fines and attorney fees that all had to be dealt with, but tomorrow was another day.

And underneath the conversation and the mundane task of eating her sandwich there'd run a current of awareness, of energy that hummed between them.

She'd felt every slide, every caress of the cotton against her skin as if it had been his touch rather than that of his clothes. She'd been devastatingly tuned in to the guarded watchfulness of his tawny eyes, the strong line of his jaw, the curve of his mouth, the nuances of his voice.

"It's this way." He brushed past her, his hip grazing her, sending a jolt through her entire body.

She followed him out of the kitchen. He opened a door to the right. "It's an odd shape."

The laundry room, a long, narrow rectangle, ran the length of the kitchen on the other side of the wall. There wasn't much room at all between the wall and the appliances. "Shared plumbing?" she guessed.

"Yeah. You got it from here?"

"Sure."

She scooted past him and raised the lid of the washing machine. She opened the dryer door. It was full of towels.

"Cade?" He turned at the door. "What do you want me to do with the towels in the dryer?"

"Damn. I forgot about those." He walked back toward her. "Here, let me get them."

She started to step out from between the appliances and the wall, he stepped in and suddenly they were wedged between the wall and the dryer, against one another. She was in full-body contact. His belt buckle pressed into her belly, one of her legs wedged between his, and her breasts pressed against his chest.

Time seemed to stop, everything distilled to the moment. His scent, the rasp of his breathing, the thud of his heart, the faint quiver that rippled through him.

"Sunny—"

"Cade—"

They went up in flames, a match thrown into tinder. He swooped his head down and took her mouth in a hard kiss, unleashing a wild, sweet abandon in her. She ground against him, her tongue mating with his. He reached beneath the edge of the T-shirt and cupped her bare bottom in his big hands. *Yes! Yes!* He pulled her hips against his and the hard ridge of his erection nudged against her lower belly. She moaned into his mouth and strained closer.

Cade kneaded and squeezed and massaged her buttocks and the frantic pace of their initial kiss gave way to a deep, drugging exchange. He skimmed his hands up over her hips and along her back to her waist. Without breaking their kiss, he lifted her, taking her on a slow, erotic ride up the hard masculine contours of his body, and depositing her atop the dryer. The metal was cool against the backs of her thighs and her bare bottom.

Sunny felt as if she were melting from the inside out. *This* was what she'd wanted, needed, craved—his touch, his scent, his taste—from the moment he'd called to her from that billboard.

He brushed his thumbs against the underside of her breasts and she gasped against his mouth, hypersensitive to even his slightest touch. Spreading her legs, she held on to his shoulders, exhilarating in the play of sleek muscle beneath her fingertips, and pulled him closer.

She dropped her head back and sighed as he wrapped his hands around her breasts and palmed the sensitive, needy tips through the thin cotton of the T-shirt. Her breasts seemed to grow and swell to a heavy ripeness under his knowing caress. It was as if Cade was tuned exactly for her body, as if he knew just the way to stroke her.

Tension mounted inside her, slicking her thighs. He weighed the fullness of her breasts in his palms and rolled and lightly plucked her taut tips between his fingers, sending pleasure spiraling through her.

She released his shoulders and braced her hands behind her, arching back, offering herself to him. With an impatient growl he swept up the T-shirt. Cool air kissed her thighs, belly and breasts. With an approving murmur, he bent over her. The stubble on his jaw rasped deliciously against her as he laved first one breast then the other with his tongue.

Her breath came in short, hard pants. His lips and tongue felt wonderful on her, but it would feel even better if he would just, please, mercy… He tugged her nipple into his wet, warm mouth and suckled. *Finally.* Sweet piercing heat arrowed through her as if there was a direct connect between her breasts and her womb. Her cries bounced off the walls in the small space as she writhed beneath the magic of his lips and tongue.

She didn't care if they didn't make it upstairs or to the sofa. She didn't care if it was here, on a dryer in a laundry room. She. Wanted. Cade. Stone.

Wrapping her legs around his waist, she rocked against his erection. “I want you,” she gasped.

He stopped and threw back his head abruptly as if she’d doused him with ice water. She’d snatch the words back in a heartbeat if she could. But the damage was done. He’d been enthralled by the same passion she had but now his eyes regained their guarded wariness. He tugged her shirt down and lifted her from the dryer. For a second she wasn’t sure if her rubbery legs would hold her upright.

“Go,” he uttered in a harsh, low tone.

She put a hand on his arm. “Cade—”

He brushed her hand away. “Go. Now.”

She didn’t see any option other than retreat.

She went.

9

THE NEXT MORNING Cade crossed the frost-brittle grass to the garage, the predawn cold bracing. Last night had been the most miserable night he could remember in a long time.

He let himself in the side door, bypassing the car area to the gym he'd set up in the back corner. Sleep had eluded him, which was something that seldom happened. He turned on the CD player and cranked the volume. Just what he needed, some good, retro, loud-ass rock and roll. The opening lines of Bon Jovi's "You Give Love a Bad Name" blasted through the garage. Good deal.

Cade snagged the jump rope off a peg. Rope work first, then the bag. He needed a hard, intense workout.

He never had trouble sleeping. He damn sure never had trouble sleeping because of a woman. Well, that wasn't strictly true. He'd lost a fair amount of sleep but that was because he was busy in bed with a woman, not because he was wallowing around totally skewed because he wanted one woman in particular. That did not happen in his world.

It had to be because she was right down the hall. Hell, he'd even decided around 3:00 a.m. that it was totally stupid to toss and turn when she was readily available. He'd climbed out of bed and made it halfway down the hall. That kiss, the look in her eyes… Seducing her wouldn't be hard or a hardship.

And then he'd heard it. It had been faint at first but grown louder as he drew closer. Sunny was snoring. It wasn't Martin's log-sawing, reverberate-through-the-house variety. This was more like a soft gentle sigh on each exhaling breath. That should've been more than enough to give him a case of limp-dick-itis.

Hell, no. He'd stood there with a hard-on feeling guilty. How could he wake her up when she was obviously sleeping so soundly? And there was a quirky vulnerability to that sound that also kept him from knocking at her door. Plus the same factor that had him sending her to her room alone in the first place. He'd brought her home with him because she'd been on the verge of making a bad decision at the end of a bad day. And then what had he done? Nearly taken her on top of the damned dryer, not exactly honorable on his part. And then lurking down the hall because he couldn't forget her honey-sweet taste against his tongue, the satin softness of her skin in his arms and beneath his lips, the intoxicating scent of her arousal, the passion glittering in her heavy-lidded eyes or the hot, sweet sounds she'd made and the near-drunk need to satisfy her flowing through his veins. He'd returned to his bed—alone—and tossed and turned the rest of the night away.

He hung up the jump rope and strapped on his gloves. "Have a Nice Day," his personal anthem, began to play. Jab right, left. Again and again he punched the bag. Last night was exactly why he avoided intense women like Sunny Templeton. She was a total pain in his ass. It should've been a simple thing. Bring her home, give her a hot shower, a square meal and a clean bed. But no, just as he'd suspected, nothing with her was simple. Everything was complicated, arousing, annoying. Maybe she'd liked his house, maybe she'd been a good listener but big damn deal. He didn't need anyone to like his house and he damn sure didn't need to talk to anyone. At least one of them wound up with a good night's sleep.

He segued into a right hook, left jab, roundhouse kick. Repeat. Hopefully Sunny was a late sleeper. He'd finish his workout, grab some breakfast and head out. With any luck she'd still be tucked safe and sound in bed and he wouldn't have to deal with her before he left.

Left hook, right jab, left roundhouse. Sweat beaded his lip. This morning he'd go after Lewis Clancy, a mean son of a bitch who wouldn't be happy to face a bond-enforcement officer bright and early after a night of hard partying.

Good.

Cade was spoiling for a fight.

SUNNY LEANED AGAINST the kitchen counter and cupped her hands around a mug of hot, fragrant coffee. Outside the window a pair of cardinals perched on a tree limb. Last night she hadn't been able to see much in the dark, but this morning, with dawn creeping over the tree line, the view was spectacular. There were no mountains or waterfalls or anything grandiose but the backyard gave way to an open meadow with a copse of trees standing beyond it.

She'd expected to sleep lousy—if at all—last night. Instead she'd settled between the crisp, cool sheets, snuggled beneath the down comforter and drifted to sleep with Cade's scent clinging to her skin and her body still humming from his touch. It had been her best night's sleep in a long time.

At the meadow's edge a rabbit delicately sniffed the morning air while a group of deer gathered at a salt block near the woods. The setting exuded tranquility, harmony, a sense of being at one with nature.

Cade emerged from the barn. Worn gray sweatpants rode low on his hips, a gray T-shirt, a good bit of it darkened with sweat, clung to his shoulders and arms. His biceps bunched like corded steel. He'd obviously been working out…hard. Sweat dripped down his neck and face in the morning sun. Mmm, mmm, mmm. So much for tranquility. So much for peace of mind. Her heart raced as if she'd just finished a marathon.

She knew the instant he saw her. His eyes locked with hers and a shiver ran through her. He came in the back door to the right of the kitchen and greenhouse, smelling like man and sweat. It was…tantalizing. Her breath hitched in her throat. Last night shimmered between them, the knowledge of what had been, the temptation of what could've been.

"You're up," he said.

She couldn't tell if he thought that was a good thing or a bad thing. In the spirit of eternal optimism, she went with the good thing. "I'm up. I'm a morning person. Thanks for finishing my laundry." She'd found her clothes neatly folded and stacked outside her door this morning. She raised the cup in his direction. "I hope you don't mind that I helped myself to a cup of coffee."

"No. I made enough for you, too," he said, blatantly ignoring her reference to the laundry. He crossed the room and poured himself a mug.

"Good coffee," she said.

He offered something between a grunt and a mutter that loosely translated to *thanks*. He was definitely in caveman mode this morning. Apparently exercise hadn't released all those feel-good endorphins for him. Or maybe it had. If that was true, he must've been scary before his workout.

What was truly scary was how bone-meltingly sexy he was first thing in the morning. The loose workout clothes coupled with his unshaven jaw and those piercing tawny eyes—it was a good look on him. Actually, she was waiting to discover a bad look.

He took a swallow of coffee. "You sleep okay?"

Not exactly gracious but that was better. "Like a log. You?"

He offered a curt nod. "Okay."

She took that for a *no*. Certainly no one could accuse him of being overly charming in the morning. She took a sip from her mug. He might be a grump but he made good coffee. Maybe he just needed an infusion of caffeine.

"I thought if I wouldn't be in the way I could make some phone calls from here this morning," Sunny said. "I need to have my cell number changed, obviously. I kept getting harassing phone calls so I finally just disconnected my home phone." Might as well make good use of his "protective custody" while she was here.

He shrugged those impossibly broad shoulders. "Suit yourself. I'll be at work."

She settled on a bar stool and watched as he opened the refrigerator and pulled out eggs, grapefruit and bread. He grabbed a skillet from a lower cabinet.

For such a large man, Cade moved around the kitchen with economy and a surprising grace. Sad but true, she could easily just sit and watch him. It was an especially nice view from behind in those sweatpants. He had some nice, tight buns going there. Which in turn cut up to a trim waist and broad, heavily-muscled shoulders. But it was the buns o' steel that truly looked fine from behind.... He turned and caught her ogling his tush. Oh well.

"Enjoying yourself?" No glimmer of humor lightened his acerbic tone.

As a matter of fact... "Immensely." She was sure she wasn't the first to admire his derriere.

Disconcertingly enough, she was equally sure she wouldn't be the last.

"Eggs, toast and grapefruit work for you? That's what I'm having. It's as easy to cook for two as it is for one."

Not a very gracious offer, but hey, someone else was making the food. Woohoo. "Sounds good. Can I do anything to help? Get plates and silverware? Cut the grapefruit?"

"No. It'll be easier if I do it. I know where everything is." He pulled a spatula out of the drawer.

"What service. I could go back upstairs if you wanted to serve me breakfast in bed." She was playing with fire. He was obviously in a pissy mood. Too bad. She was in a smart-ass flirty mood. She'd woken up that way. Amazing what a good night's sleep could do for a gal.

Cade looked at her, a dangerous glint in his eye. "If I was serving you breakfast in bed, it wouldn't be eggs and toast." The low growl in his voice stirred a primal heat deep within her.

Oh. My. Well, that proved it. She could be utterly, absolutely turned on with just a look and a tone.

He cracked an egg into a bowl and she swallowed hard. Guess he was still serving eggs and she could forget about the other. For now.

"You snore," he said, glancing over his shoulder.

"What?" Here she was all hot and bothered and he had to go say that.

"You snore." He beat the eggs into a froth.

"I do not. Anyway, how would you know? I was all the way down the hall."

He raised a dark eyebrow. "Exactly. I could hear you all the way down the hall."

"No one's ever mentioned it before."

"Because you date pansy-asses and they're too much of a wuss to mention it." He dropped the bread into the toaster and stirred the eggs into the skillet.

"I do not date pansy-asses," she shot back. Well, maybe compared to him. Everything was relative. "And how would you know, anyway?"

"I can tell."

"You're confusing wuss with gentleman." She smiled sweetly over the rim of her coffee cup. "Of course, I can see how you'd have trouble making the distinction, since you're not intimately acquainted with gentlemanly behavior. A gentleman doesn't threaten to throw a woman over his shoulder and tote her out of a public domain." Her pulse fluttered at the thought. "And if I snored, a gentleman wouldn't be so rude as to point it out."

He neatly sliced the grapefruit in half. "You should come with a pair of earplugs."

He spooned up the eggs and put half a grapefruit and a piece of toast on each plate. He plunked a plate down in front of her.

"Thank you," she said automatically.

"You're welcome." He sat on his stool, picked up his fork and began to eat.

Sunny broke off a piece of toast and scooped a forkful of egg onto it. Seeing as how he was already surly, she might as well dive right in.

"So, is some irate girlfriend going to show up today, demanding to know why I'm here?" She *did* need to know and she was damn curious as to the state of his love life. Sure he'd kissed her last night but girlfriends—heck, wives—wouldn't stop a lot of guys from making that move or more. She popped the morsel into her mouth. Yum. Sourdough toast and good eggs.

He forked the last spoonful of his eggs into his mouth, his grapefruit and toast still untouched. Oh, boy. One of those one-food-at-a-time people. He finished chewing and swallowed.

"You're safe. I don't date during the holidays. It avoids any awkwardness over presents."

After a stunned moment, Sunny said, "You cheap bastard." This guy was incredible.

It was his turn to look stunned. "Did you just call me a cheap bastard?"

"I did."

He laughed. She didn't see what was so funny. "It's not the money," he said, spooning out a section of grapefruit. "It's the whole gift thing. If you give a present, the woman thinks you're serious. If you don't give a present then she feels slighted. Either way, you're screwed." He worked through the grapefruit methodically as if it were a mission to be accomplished.

"Now there's a dose of the holiday spirit. And I can tell you're a true romantic." She'd already picked up on his attitude last night when he'd commented on his brother's engagement.

"Here's the bottom line. I've dated some women I've never slept with—" *that was hard to believe* "—and I've slept with women I've never dated—" *uh-huh, sounded closer to the truth* "—and then there's the crossover—" *probably precious little* "—but I'm particular in all departments." *Big tits. Little brains. No backbone.* "I don't have trouble lining up either one—" *arrogant* "—but I'm not the Memphis gigolo, either." *Right.* "And for what it's worth I don't date or sleep with more than one woman at a time and they know exactly what to expect going in." *Give him a gold star.*

He'd finished eating. He turned around on the stool and leaned back, bracing his elbows on the counter. It threw his broad chest and drum-tight abs into distracting relief beneath his shirt and seemed to suck all the air out of her lungs. She drew a deep breath. That was better.

"And what should the lucky chosen one expect going in?" *Extraordinary sex?*

"Are you—" His tawny eyes held a sensual heat that unleashed a hot river of want in her.

She'd been ready to jump into that fire last night, but now, with the rational light of day, she needed to have a better idea of exactly what to expect…if she decided to go there. "Strictly rhetorical. You know I have that pansy-ass affinity." Sweet sanity but he had nice arms—dark hair sprinkling his forearms, well-formed biceps. She curled her toes around the stool's metal-rod footrest.

"How disappointing." His eyes held a watchfulness that was both exciting and disconcerting.

"I'm sure you're devastated. I'm also sure you'll manage to recover. You strike me as resilient. And I'm waiting with bated breath to know what a woman can expect from you."

"I have a four-week policy. I don't see anyone for more than four weeks. It keeps things clean and simple."

He actually seemed serious. "For whom?"

"For everyone."

"I take it you don't believe in love." Sunny was

vaguely disappointed that Cade was just another bachelor too cynical for love.

"I firmly believe in love. I just don't want any part of it."

"Please. You can't stop there. Because…?"

"Falling in love is like skydiving with a malfunctioning parachute. Sooner or later you come down and hit the ground." She caught a glimmer of something in his eye. "I just prefer not to ever jump out of the plane." He levered himself off of the stool and stood.

"Is that what you tell all your potential girlfriends?"

He rounded the counter into the kitchen. "I spare them the analogy. We just go over the four weeks."

"So, you just announce, 'You've got me for four weeks,' and they say, 'Okay'?" Why in the world would any woman agree to that? A fork clattered to the tile floor and he bent over to pick it up, the sweatpants clinging to his fine male booty. *Come on, Sunny, you know exactly why women would agree to that,* a nagging little voice inside her chided.

He straightened and shrugged, putting the fork into the dishwasher. "Pretty much."

Was he calculating or just brutally honest? "That's brilliant on your part."

"I wouldn't say brilliant." A faint frown furrowed his forehead. "More along the line of fair."

He really, truly didn't get it. "Ha. It's more like waving a red flag at a bull. I'm guessing every one of them has vowed to be the one that'll drive you to break your four-week rule." A ridiculous jealousy arrowed through her. They probably catered to his every whim, jumped at his every command, each one of them trying to prove in that four-week span that he couldn't live without them come week five. Blech. She didn't want any more breakfast. She pushed her plate across the counter to him. "Thanks, it was good. Whether you know it or not, you're the ultimate dating challenge for them."

"Maybe that's just your take on it."

Men! "Trust me. That's exactly what all women think."

"What about you? Are you inspired to make me break my four-week rule?"

She wasn't sure whether that was a challenge or an invitation. Either way, wasn't this what she wanted? Her body screamed a resounding yes. Her brain, thank goodness, was still working and uttered a quiet yet emphatic negative. Not on those terms. "I don't think so. I don't do well without Christmas presents." She stood and pushed her stool in. "I like to both give and receive. I can't see that it would work out well for either one of us."

SUNNY PUT ASIDE the to-do list and stood up from the bar stool when she heard Cade coming down the stairs. She'd brushed her teeth and then headed back downstairs while he showered and dressed. Having an entire floor separating them while he was naked struck her as a very prudent move.

"I've got a quick question for you," she said. "Do you have a computer with an Internet connection I could use?" Hey, he was the one who'd bundled her out of her house last night without any of her stuff, even though in retrospect it had been a wise choice not to drop her at Joanie's or the dive bar.

He nodded toward the den. "Laptop with Wi-Fi connection's in there. So's the TV."

She'd skip the TV but the laptop with a Wi-Fi. Nice. "Thanks. So, you're working a case today?" Sunny said.

"Yep. That's what I do," he said, walking toward her.

Sunny leaned against the kitchen doorjamb, determined to be civil even though it seemed beyond him. Decked out head to toe in black, showered but unshaved, he epitomized a badass in a bad mood.

"Do you ever let people ride along with you? Not that I'm asking to go," she tacked on at his don't-even-friggin'-think-about-it scowl. "I've got plenty of work to do myself. I was just curious."

"No. I work alone. Linc and I occasionally pair up." He opened a small door on the side of the stairs that she hadn't noticed before.

"I thought bounty hunters rode shotgun together a lot." The door revealed a coat/storage closet beneath the stairs.

"You've been reading those Stephanie Plum books or watching *Dog the Bounty Hunter* on TV."

"I like the Plum books. Stephanie and Lulu make a good team." Stephanie and Morelli made an even better pair. Stephanie and Ranger? That was trouble.

"I don't know. Never read them. My sister does. They're just characters in a book."

Well, she supposed he didn't need to read about fictional characters when he lived it every day.

He tugged his shirt over his head and she didn't even pretend not to stare. If he was stripping, she was looking. No harm in looking, well, except to her pulse rate.

Broad shoulders, broad chest with just the right amount of hair scattered over it and down his belly so that he looked like a real man but not so much that he looked like monkey man, trim waist, nice flat six-pack abs. Sweet mercy. Sunny figured she was lucky she didn't puddle on the floor at his feet. Altogether it was a knee-weakening expanse of smooth skin except for a small puckered scar on his side.

She'd seen shirtless men before. But none so well-built in such close proximity before. She desperately searched for a brain cell to find a conversational topic.

"How'd you get that scar?"

He pulled a white vest off of a closet hook. "An FTA with a gun got off a lucky shot. Fortunately, he had bad aim. Now, depending on the case, I don't leave home without this." He put it on and velcroed it into place. "Kevlar."

"Has it ever stopped a bullet before?" The thought made her faintly nauseous.

He grinned. "A couple of times." He pulled the shirt back over his head and tucked it into his pants.

Next came a shoulder holster complete with a very lethal-looking gun. She swallowed as he buckled the holster on. Then he clipped on a small canister of mace and what looked like a gun but had a funny cartridge on the front around his waist.

"What's that?"

"Taser."

Next came handcuffs. Her heart pounded, this time for an altogether different reason. He looked very macho suited out like that. Who knew she had such an…affinity for macho? Cade Stone was hell on her blood pressure.

"You wear this stuff every day?"

"Definitely not. It depends on the cases I'm working."

"This case you're going on, it's dangerous?"

"Dangerous is a relative term. You could consider it dangerous to leave your house."

"It was yesterday. So then on a relative scale, how dangerous is this case or is there a privacy issue where you can't discuss it?"

He shrugged into the leather bomber jacket he'd worn last night. "No privacy issues. They skip bail and it's public knowledge. This morning I'm looking for Lewis Clancy. Lewis didn't bother to show up at court two days ago on an Assault and Battery." He closed the closet door.

"Assault and Battery?"

"Lewis has a nasty temper and a worse disposition." Cade's smile was a feral baring of teeth, a predator preparing for the hunt. An answering heat stirred in her. "His girlfriend expected him to show up because she's the one that posted his bail in the first place, but Lewis was a no-show. Not only is he a mean SOB, he's a player. The bail-posting girlfriend eagerly spilled the new girl's address. Lewis will be piled up in bed, sleeping off a hard night of partying." Cade's lip curled in a not-nice smile. "He won't be happy to see me."

Sunny tried to swallow some of her trepidation. Now all of sudden Cade didn't look quite as invincible as he had two minutes ago. "How old is Lewis? How big?"

"Twenty-six and a little bigger than me, but I can take him. You don't need to worry about me."

"Maybe I'm worried about Lewis." Liar. "You're pretty tricked out there."

"When I go in, I like to go in ready." He picked a pair of sunglasses off the small table that butted up to the staircase. "I'll pull a car out of the garage for you. It's a beater that I drive in on snow days when I don't want to chance the 'Vette. I'll leave the keys in it. If you take it, try not to ram anyone today." He could've kept that sarcastic comment to himself. "Help yourself to whatever you want in the fridge or the pantry."

He turned toward the front door and she followed him.

"When should I expect you back?" The later, the better, as far as she was concerned. She just wasn't sure exactly when she should start to be concerned.

"Missing me already?"

"Hardly. Just curious as to how long I get to have your fabulous house to myself."

"Late afternoon. Early evening."

If the guy with a bad temper didn't knife him or shoot him first.

"Um, try not to get yourself killed today. It'd be really weird for me to be here if you get yourself dead."

"When you put it that way, I'll try extrahard to avoid being killed. I'd hate to carry around eternal guilt over inconveniencing you."

"I'd appreciate it." And because she didn't know what else to do, she shook his hand. His hand practically swallowed hers and a tingle shot up her arm.

A frown creased his forehead. "What's that for?"

"It's for good luck and a thank you. I'm not sure that I've said thank you and I should. You know…for everything." Yeah, he wasn't exactly prince charming but he had rescued her after a fashion yesterday, not that she'd asked for nor particularly wanted rescuing, thank you very much. But he had brought her into his home and for all that he was gruff and surly, at least no photographers were peering in the windows at her.

"Surely you can do better than that." It came out as a sexy drawl that seriously undermined her common sense.

He planted his hands on the door behind her, trapping her between him and the front door. Well, not exactly trapping because they both knew she could easily duck beneath his arm and away…if she wanted to. But God help her, she seemed to have totally abandoned all semblance of reason because she didn't want to escape.

Heat rushed through her, tightening her nipples into hard anticipation, pooling into a wet warmth between her thighs.

He lowered his head. "If I get sloppy today and don't make it back home, I'd like to take more than a handshake with me to my final reward."

She, who'd always liked her men somewhat "tame," was incredibly turned on by the ruthless element of the hunter. He made her hot. The gun, the handcuffs, the taser and the mace. The Kevlar jacket. The whole I'm-a-badass package left her wet and quivering for his touch.

He kissed her. Hard, fast but thorough. Only his mouth had touched her, but her entire body was on fire.

"Sunny." His breath stirred against her cheek. She opened her eyes. His expression remained inscrutable, but his eyes smoldered. "Last night you slept alone because you'd had a hell of a day and I'd promised myself I'd keep you safe. When I get back today, I can take you home, I can take you to a friend's, or you can stay here." His gaze slid over her like a lover's touch. "But you won't sleep alone." His husky voice was almost hypnotic. "And I can't guarantee you'll get much sleep."

She moistened her lips. "Four weeks?"

He inclined his dark head. "Four weeks."

"What about Christmas? The no-holiday hiatus."

He trailed his finger along her jaw, wreaking further havoc with her pulse. "I'm willing to make an exception. Plus, you know the deal. Your choice."

"And if I say no?" She tried to focus on the conversation rather than the mesmerizing heat in his eyes and his touch.

"You could say no." He leaned in and nuzzled the same path his finger had taken along her jaw, his mouth warm and sensuous, his stubble a delicious rasp against her skin. He trailed kisses down her neck and she slanted her head to the side, biting back a moan. He closed his hand around one of her breasts and brushed his thumb over her stiff peak. He gently nipped the sensitive juncture of her shoulder and neck and she cried out, her whole body trembling with desire. He straightened and dropped his hand to his side. "But we both know you won't."

Sunny was still dazed when he closed the door behind him.

10

"I HOPE THE OTHER GUY LOOKS WORSE," Linc said with a laugh when Cade walked into AA Atco a couple of hours later.

"Trust me, he does," Cade said. Lewis Clancy had landed a kick that busted open Cade's right eyebrow. By the time Cade had wrestled him into cuffs, Clancy was very, very sorry.

Marlene hurried over to fuss over Cade. "That needs to be stitched up."

"Stitches are for pansy-asses," Martin said, rumbling out of his office.

"He needs stitches." Marlene stood her ground.

Cade ignored them both and headed to the bathroom. He closed the door behind him.

"Do you need any help?" Marlene asked from the other side.

"No. I'm fine." Blood had dried over his eye and down the side of his face. He grimaced in the mirror. He looked like he'd just had his ass kicked.

It could've been worse considering he'd found Clancy still strung out on crystal meth.

Cade grabbed a couple of paper towels and washed the dried blood off with cold water. What would Sunny say when she saw his face? Would she make a fuss over him? Offer to get him an ice pack, make a big deal over him getting hurt in the first place? He'd sensed her concern this morning, read it in her eyes.

He'd thought about her all morning. Even when he was busting Clancy, she'd been in the back of his mind. Want for her gnawed like a constant ache inside him, too strong to ignore.

He opened the mirror-fronted medicine cabinet. They kept a well-stocked first-aid kit for just this type of thing. He washed out the cut with hydrogen peroxide—that stung like a son of a bitch—applied antibiotic cream, and closed the cut with three butterfly bandages. Good enough.

When he came out of the bathroom, Linc was gone and Marlene was on the phone. Cade strolled into Martin's office, closing the door behind him.

Martin looked up from a crossword puzzle. "You knocked?"

Cade chose not to sit. Instead he leaned against the doorjamb. He cut straight to the point. "Marlene isn't a good idea."

Martin casually leaned back in his chair and propped his booted feet on his worn desk. He clasped his hands behind his head and pretended to study the ceiling. Finally he looked at Cade, beetling his eyebrows in mock perplexity. "Funny. I don't recall asking you. Anyway, it's a little like closing the gate after the horse is out of the barn isn't it?"

Cade kept his face expressionless. Martin wasn't going to get the best of his temper. "I distinctly recall Marlene mentioning not being cut out for casual sex. You were there."

"Marlene's a big girl. She can make her own decisions." He folded his hands over his still-flat belly.

Cade made a split decision, based on years of dealing with the old man. Appealing to Martin's vested interests would be much more effective than appealing to his sense of rightness because Martin wrote his own rules in that department. "We need her here, Martin. We've always been careful not to mix business and pleasure. We can't afford for her to walk out when this is over." Sunny's comment that the four-week rule would entice most women to prove it wrong echoed in his head. He'd never thought of it that way, but unfortunately, that had Marlene written all over it. He didn't want to see Martin break her heart.

"Son—" Cade gritted his teeth; he was damn sure Martin called him that just to remind him of his paternity "—this is none of your business."

"Marlene is my business." Cade smiled and he knew it wasn't pleasant. "If you hurt her, I'm going to scatter your ass from one end of Poplar to the other."

Martin rolled a pen between his fingers. "You've been looking for a reason for a long time."

"Don't give me one now."

"You could give me a little credit," Martin said without any of his usual bluster, suddenly looking every year of his age.

It was an overture.

Cade ignored it. He'd learned to be strong a long time ago. "You'd have to earn it first."

Cade turned on his heel.

"Close the door on your way out," Martin said with a quiet weariness from behind him. Cade walked out, pulling the door closed until it clicked.

Marlene was elbow-deep in the file cabinet, one of the never-ending aspects of her job. She looked over her shoulder at Cade. She frowned at his patched brow.

"You probably needed stitches but I'll save my breath. How'd it go last night? How's Sunny? What's she like?"

Sexy. Mouthy. Distracting. And for the next four weeks…his. "She's a pain in the ass."

Marlene quirked an inquiring brow.

"There was a little problem last night when I dropped her off at her house."

"Oh dear. What kind of problem?"

He gave her a quick recap of the events at Sunny's house, leaving out him carrying her from and to the car and their kiss. "I tried to drop her off at your place."

Marlene closed the file drawer with a snap. "If you came by you saw Martin's truck at my house." She looked him dead in the eye.

"Marlene, he—"

She stayed him with an upheld hand. "I know who he is and what he is, Cade. We'll keep it out of the office but after hours, our time is our own. I don't think he'll break my heart, but if he does that's a chance I have to take. I know you're concerned about me and I appreciate it."

He raked a frustrated hand over his head. "What happened to the Internet dating?"

"It did exactly what it was supposed to—it got Martin's attention. And now I've got four weeks." She actually winked at him.

Suddenly one of the components that had been an essential part of his life for a long time seemed to not make nearly as much sense as it used to—that damn four-week rule. And he wasn't altogether too certain that he shouldn't be more concerned about Martin in this deal than Marlene. He had a feeling Martin might've just met his match.

Cade nodded. There wasn't much to say to that.

Marlene's smile thanked him for letting it go. "So, finish the story. What'd you wind up doing with Sunny?"

"I brought her home with me," he said with a nonchalant shrug.

Marlene's mouth gaped and then snapped shut. A coy smile bloomed on her face. "Really?"

"Really."

"And where is she now?"

"My house."

"Well, that'll be interesting. Gracie stopped by about an hour ago. She left Prudence in the flower shop and she was heading out to your place to get the Christmas decorations up. I bet they'll have a nice visit."

Sunny at his house. Gracie, the Mouth of the South, showing up. Marlene and Martin. Why'd everything have to be so complicated?

SUNNY SAT CROSS-LEGGED on the sofa cushion that she'd dragged into the sunroom area, Cade's laptop resting on her thighs, a fire crackling cheerily in the fireplace. The fireplace was obviously used and there was a stack of wood to the left of the hearth, so she'd built a fire after taking a brisk walk this morning. She'd had to find a momentary outlet for all that energy bottled inside her after he left. He was right. She'd be in his bed tonight. But it'd be on her terms.

She checked off the first item on her to-do list. She now had a new phone number. Her service might be spotty due to a weak signal now and then, but it had only taken about fifteen minutes to change her cell number.

Next a conversation with her attorney. Celia Mallard's secretary put her on hold. Sunny considered it a good sign she'd actually caught Celia in the office.

The on-hold Muzak ended and Celia was on the other line. "Sunny, I tried calling earlier and it went straight to voice mail."

Sunny offered a quick rundown and gave Celia her new number.

"Well, good news this morning. It looks as if they're dropping the felony charges and it should be reduced to a traffic violation. If that's the case you'll still have to appear at court and you're probably looking at a stiff fine, but absolutely no jail time. I'm waiting to hear from Cecil's attorney."

Sunny sagged with relief. She could figure out how to pay a fine. She hadn't been sure how she'd handle her house and her business if she had even a couple of months in jail. "That's fantastic. How…why?"

Celia laughed. "Santa came early for you this year. Remember the guy in the Santa suit who helped you out of your car?"

"Distinctly. His beard had gotten knocked to one side."

"Well, he saw Cecil's interview on last night's news and it bothered him because Cecil was presenting a very slanted accounting. Meeks claimed he didn't see you until he had passed you. Santa, however, saw him wave before he ever got to you. In light of Santa's willingness to testify on your behalf and the fact that now Cecil can look magnanimous by dropping the charges, I'm almost certain they'll be dropped."

"Should I talk to the press or—"

"No. Do just what you're doing. Keep a low profile until we hear from Cecil. Let him think he's won."

They settled a few remaining details and ended the call. The first person she thought about sharing the good news with was Cade. He might not win any charm awards, but he'd gone out of his way to take care of her last night. However, the only way she knew to get in touch with him was to call the bail bond office and that just felt…weird. She'd tell him when he got back.

She forced herself to work through the rest of the to-do list. She transferred the bail bond fee from her account into Nadine's. She called for information on getting her car out of the impound lot and she e-mailed two clients about design specifics for their Web sites.

Sunny checked off the last item on her list and then e-mailed the notes she made regarding the various items to herself. She stood and stretched. She'd just got herself into a downward dog position when a delivery van pulled up to the back door.

After her initial start of surprise, she saw Gracie's Flowers scripted on the side. Gracie? Sunny was almost sure that's what Cade had called his sister.

A petite blonde hurried out of the driver's side, opened the van's rear door and pulled out a box. Yep, she had to be his sister because she was tiny and Sunny definitely was a Sasquatch in comparison.

Sunny stood next to the cushion she'd dragged

into the greenhouse, unsure exactly what to do. It wasn't her house so greeting the woman at the door didn't feel right.

The woman unlocked the back door and walked in, carrying the box in front of her.

"Uh, hi," Sunny said.

The woman screamed, jumped, and promptly dropped the box.

"I'm sorry. I'm sorry," Sunny said, she held up her hands. "I'm harmless."

The woman glanced from Sunny to where she'd nested in the sunroom and back to Sunny and smiled, obviously deciding she was neither a deranged killer nor a burglar.

"Holy hell, you scared me."

"I didn't mean to," Sunny said, wincing. "That's why I said something. I didn't think you saw me standing here. By the way, I'm Sunny Templeton." She stepped forward, offering her hand and a smile. "You must be Gracie."

She wasn't sure she'd catch the family resemblance if she passed the other woman on the street but it was there. Granted, Cade was huge with darker hair and this woman was petite with blond curly hair, and Gracie's eyes were sky-blue where Cade's were tawny, but if you looked closely the shape and set of their eyes was the same.

They also shared a similar mouth and a slightly square chin.

Gracie kept her distance, her blue eyes puzzled. "How'd you know my name?"

Sunny gestured outside. "It says it on the side of your van."

"Duh." Gracie laughed and smacked her forehead with the heel of her hand. "Yeah. I'm Gracie Stone." She closed the gap between them and clasped Sunny's hand in a quick, firm handshake. "Nice to meet you. That's why you look familiar. You're the lady on the flyer, the one that hit Cecil Meeks yesterday."

Sunny waggled her fingers. "That's me."

Gracie moved the box over to the counter, the scent of fresh evergreen perfuming the air. "I don't mean to be rude but how in the heck did you wind up here? I mean, Cade actually knows you're here, right?" She propped against the counter, radiating curiosity.

Did women regularly show up at his house uninvited? "He does. He brought me here last night."

"Holy hell."

That seemed to be one of her favorite expressions. "I beg your pardon?"

"You spent the night here?"

Sunny wasn't prone to blushing but heat swept

her face. "I…uh…stayed in the guest room." *But you won't be tonight,* a wicked little voice whispered in her head.

A grin spread over Gracie's face that looked so much like Cade's a funny feeling blossomed in Sunny's chest. "Well. Hope springs eternal."

Sunny wasn't quite sure what to make of that cryptic comment. Was it because she'd spent the night or because she'd slept in the guest room? She must've looked perplexed.

"Cade's lived here for over ten years and he's never brought a woman out here. All his dating is strictly off-site. You must be special."

Sunny wasn't quite sure how to respond to that. They weren't dating. They weren't lovers…yet. "We're not—he bailed me out last night."

She nodded, her mouth quirked in a rueful smile. "I saw the news last night. But how'd you wind up here?" She laughed. "Oops. I bet you're getting there. I have a tendency to interrupt. My bad."

Sunny laughed along with her. Gracie Stone was like a little human minitornado but her good humor was infectious. For a brief, awful moment, the traitorous thought crossed Sunny's mind that it would've been nice if Nadine was a little more like Gracie and a little less like…well, Nadine. "It's sort of complicated. He took me home—"

"Cade took you home?" Gracie looked as if she'd announced he took a spaceship to Mars.

"He was just giving me a ride." How the heck did she explain last night's events? She settled on the abbreviated version. "It gets complicated from there, but I wound up here." Okay, it just sounded weird and secretive when put that way.

"The company bails out lots of people and he never brings any of *them* home with him." Gracie appeared quite smug.

"It was sort of a protective custody thing," Sunny said, borrowing Cade's phrase from last night. It sounded better than telling his sister he'd all but kidnapped her.

Gracie smiled, her blue eyes twinkling. "Okay, if you say so."

Sunny didn't particularly like that smile. "He says I'm a pain in the ass," she blurted.

Gracie grinned but said nothing. That was the wrong response. Sunny tried again. "He threatened to throw me over his shoulder and carry me out of the police station yesterday."

Gracie nodded. "He would've, too. He's used to being in charge. You should've seen him with my boyfriend when I was in high school. Mark was scared to death of him. I always got home early.

When I was a teenager I was convinced I was going to die a virgin."

Sunny busted out laughing but shot her a sympathetic look. She couldn't imagine a seventeen-year-old boy having to face Cade's unyielding stare.

Gracie laughed along with her. "That's just who and what Cade is—it's as natural to him as breathing. Most of the time he has all the finesse of a linebacker, but he's got a good heart."

"I can see that." The finesse of a linebacker? Definitely. The good heart? He'd shielded her from the reporters and paparazzi and her own misguided notions when he didn't have to, fed her and gave her a place to stay.

"So, how long are you here?"

That was the burning question. She was playing it by ear. A lot depended on how negotiable he was when he showed up. "Just until things die down."

For a few seconds Gracie wore a peculiar expression, as if she'd checked out of the conversation. She shook her head and smiled at Sunny as if she possessed a secret, then pushed away from the counter. "Well, I better get busy 'cause I'm burning daylight. The house isn't going to decorate itself. You can either pretend I'm not here or you can help if you want."

Ignoring Gracie Stone seemed as improbable as

ignoring her brother and she liked the woman's outgoing personality.

"I can help."

Sunny grabbed her shoes and jacket and together they unloaded mountains of fragrant greenery—cedar, pine, prickly holly and blue-spruce trimmings—and finally two fresh trees, which they placed in stands.

"That's it," Gracie announced, brushing her hands together. "Now we can start decorating the house."

Sunny kicked off her shoes and pulled off her coat. "Okay. Tell me what to do."

"We'll do the greenery first and the trees last," Gracie said.

Gracie kept up an ongoing stream of conversation while she worked on the mantel over the dining room fireplace. "I do Daddy's and Cade's houses every year for the holidays—otherwise neither one of them would bother. Cade likes it all decorated, but it's just not in him."

Nope. She couldn't see him decking his halls with boughs of holly. Sunny watched in amazement as Gracie twisted and tweaked pine and cedar into place on the rough-hewn mantel. Sunny could put together a jam-up Web site or design and construct intricate stained-glass pieces, but she was terrible at stuff like this.

"Hey, hand me some of that holly—a big piece with lots of berries," Gracie said.

Sunny handed it off and Gracie continued her magic. "That looks great," Sunny said.

"Thanks. Me and Linc are artistic like our Mama was—she did the painting in here and up in the guest room. Cade's like Daddy, which is why they bump heads. They're too much alike. Linc did this." She gestured to a piece of pottery on the mantel.

Sunny traced her finger along the rounded, curved piece fired in shades of purple and green. "Very nice. Very sensual."

Gracie nodded. "Linc's good. He lives in a loft downtown. Needless to say he does his own decorating. He does a great retro, silver-tinsel tree with colored lights—very funky. Have you met Linc?" Gracie asked, moving to the hall banister where she began to twine greenery. Sunny shook her head now because she didn't think she could get a word in edgewise. "No? You'll like him. Everybody likes Linc."

"He's a bounty hunter, too, isn't he?" she managed to slip in.

"Bond-enforcement agent," Gracie corrected. "Yep. I'm the only one not involved in the business. I got my horticultural and business degree a couple of years ago and then last year Cade helped me start my florist business."

Sunny noticed it was Cade and not their father who'd helped launch Gracie's business. Interesting. The same as it had been Cade rather than their father who'd culled her dates. "Do you like having your own business?"

They spent the next several hours hanging wreaths, stringing greenery and decorating the trees—one in the dining room corner, the other in the front window of the den to the left of the front door. By the time they were through, not only did the house look and smell fantastic—Sunny was inspired to get her own decorations out and up when she got home—but she felt as if she knew the Stone family intimately and they were an interesting bunch.

Gracie had entertained her with stories about herself and her fiancé Mark Fletcher's romance, how Georgia had tagged along with Linc and they'd fallen in love. She knew Linc played the guitar and Cade spent his spare time restoring cars. Cade had joined the family business immediately out of high school but had insisted on, and helped pay for, Linc's and Gracie's college education.

While they'd covered the trees in ornaments that spanned nearly forty years—macaroni-noodle angels made by them in kindergarten, Popsicle-stick-framed Christmas photos—Gracie touched on how difficult it had been after their mother died, how their father had had a total breakdown.

And in all the stories, it was always Cade that came up as the strong one, the alpha, the leader of the pack.

By the time Gracie packed her van, Sunny knew the Stones were close in a way her family never had been and never would be.

Gracie gave her a quick hug. "I've had the best time with you today. This was a lot more fun, and a lot faster, than if I did it all myself."

"I enjoyed it. It was great meeting you. I definitely know who I'm calling the next time I need flowers delivered."

"Definitely. I'll take care of you." Gracie paused on her way out the door. "The AA Atco Christmas party's here next Friday night." The one The Best Barbecue was catering with…pork. "I'll see you then."

"That's nice of you to invite me but I'm not an employee."

"Minor point." Gracie shot her a cheeky look as she ducked out the back door. "You'll be there."

11

CADE GARAGED THE 'VETTE and the beater he'd pulled out for Sunny before he'd left in the morning, relieved Gracie's van wasn't in the drive. He wasn't in the mood to deal with his sister, even though he appreciated her taking the time to decorate the house. He could've worked at least one more case but he wasn't in the mood to deal with an FTA. It was midafternoon and for the first time in a long time—make that *ever*—he'd quit early with no plans to work any more today. The rest of the day was about Sunny. He slid the barn doors closed. Who was he kidding? The whole day had been about her. He hadn't been able to get her out of his head.

He crossed to the back door. He had a feeling he'd find her in the back of the house. Brittle grass crunched beneath his feet and wood-smoke curled from the chimney, adding a tangy scent to the day's crispness. The cold air stung the split over his eye.

Cade walked in through the door to a fire

burning in the hearth and the scent of evergreens. Sunny uncurled herself from a cushion, obviously "borrowed" from the couch, on the sunroom floor. It should've been intrusive to have her in his house. Instead it was *nice* to walk in to this, to her.

"Hi." Her smile and her eyes held a mix of welcome, challenge and sexual heat.

"Hi," he said, noting the way her jeans hugged her hips and her sweater skimmed the curve of her breasts.

He shrugged out of his jacket and tossed it onto one of the bar stools. Her gaze trailed over him and his body tightened as if she'd touched him.

She eyed the bandage over his eyebrow. "I see you managed to not get yourself killed today. That's a plus."

"I'm considerate that way. I didn't want to inconvenience you. You should see the other guy." He advanced on her.

"No, thanks." She frowned. "Does it hurt?"

He smiled and trapped her against the counter. She smelled like sun-warmed woman—his woman. The air between them felt heated, charged, like the precursor to a summer storm. "If I say yes, will you make it better?"

"Do I look like Florence Nightingale?"

A smattering of freckles across her nose, a keen

intelligence in her eyes, and a mouth that smiled as readily as it argued, she looked like exactly what would make him feel better. "I'd say a dead ringer."

Sunny reached up and feathered her fingers along the outer edges of the bandage, her touch gossamer-light but still sending a shaft of want through him. "It's swollen."

"You have no idea." One touch and he was hard for her. He tangled his hands in her hair, burying his fingers in its thick softness, and her eyes darkened at his touch.

"You're staying," he said. It wasn't a question.

She slid her hands along his neck and clasped them behind his head. "I'm still trying to decide," she murmured huskily.

"I'll buy you a Christmas present."

"You think I can be bought?" Amusement gleamed in her eyes.

"I sincerely hope so."

Her lips parted and her eyes searched his.

He didn't try to mask his hunger for her. He couldn't, even if he wanted to. He'd never felt desperate for a woman. What the hell was it about *her* that tied him up in knots? Who knew? He only knew he wanted her. Needed her. And he meant to have her.

She uttered a soft sigh and pulled his mouth down to hers. He kissed her like a man who'd stumbled on an oasis in the middle of a desert trek. Instead of quenching the fire raging inside him, the softness of her lips, the play of her tongue against his, the taste of her mouth fanned the flames licking at him.

"About that present…I want something nice," she murmured against his mouth, sliding her hands over his shoulders. She caught his lower lip between hers and sucked gently, a long, slow pull.

"I've got something nice right here for you." He shifted against her.

"Neanderthal," she said as she rubbed against him, her eyes agleam. "Expensive."

"Expensive?"

"Mmm. Think of all the money you've saved over the years," she teased and leaned into him. The stiff tips of her nipples stabbed at his chest through their clothes. His cock stirred against her belly.

"How expensive?" He nuzzled her neck, inhaling the scent of her hair, her skin. She canted her head to the side, allowing him unfettered access. He slid his tongue along the soft flesh and she trembled against him.

Her lips found his jaw, her fingers the rigid line of his cock. "Don't make me call you a cheap bastard again."

She stroked up the length of him through his

jeans and every ounce of blood in his body gathered there to experience the rush of her touch. "Expensive, then," he said. Whatever she wanted, it was hers. At that moment he would probably trade his soul to the devil to have her.

He scooped her up and tossed her over his shoulder, her delicious ass next to his cheek, her breasts pressed against his shoulder.

"I'm perfectly capable of walking up the stairs," she said, breathless but without any real protest as he strode down the hall.

She could say what she wanted to say, he'd seen the heat in her eyes and he'd guaran-damn-tee none of the men she'd ever known had carried her anywhere.

"I'm sure you are." He took the stairs two at a time.

"I suppose I should again be thankful you're not dragging me by my hair." Her wry humor delivered in a sexy, breathless rush was heady stuff.

He smiled at the back of her knees. Even he knew that would be taking it too far. "I told you before, your hair's too short to drag you."

He walked into his room and tossed her onto the bed. He traced the delicate, elegant indention of her ankle with his fingertips and her violet eyes grew smoky.

"You know the deal," he said. "Four weeks." They'd talked about the four-week thing this morning, maybe yesterday. Sometime. All he could think about was the press of her body against his, which was now absent, her scent, the way she'd taste, the sound of her sighs, the reverberation of his name when she came.

"New day, new deal." She smiled sexily from where she lay sprawled across his mattress. "No four-week plan."

This wasn't the way it was supposed to go. She'd misunderstood. "There's always a four-week plan."

She rolled to her side and propped on one elbow, tugging her sweater down where it had slid up. "Not this time. Any woman who agrees to that is either desperate or stupid and I've never considered myself either."

Another woman would've begun to undress, would've flashed some skin to reinforce the issue. Dammit, why'd she have to be so contrary? And why'd he still want her with a throbbing ache?

Because Sunny was…Sunny. Unlike any woman he'd ever known before.

"You're not giving me a choice." He sent her a glare that left most grown men trembling.

She laughed, a low sensual sound that feathered

down his spine like a lover's touch. "There's always a choice."

"I'm the one making all the concessions." No four-week safety net. A damn present, expensive at that, for Christmas. "What do I get out of this?" She arched an amused eyebrow. "Besides the obvious."

A slow smile curved her mouth and ricocheted through him. "You—" she rolled to her back "—get to throw out the rules and know what it's like—" she stretched her arms over her head, arching her back, her nipples outlined against her sweater "—to not be caged by four weeks." She rolled to her knees and knelt on the bed, facing him across the expanse, challenging him. "You get to run free."

CADE STOOD POISED BY THE BED, nostrils flared, eyes narrowed, and time stretched like an eternity between them. Would her wolf turn and run away from her or choose to run with her?

He pulled off his shoulder holster, gun still in it, and placed it on the floor. "No four weeks," he conceded.

Finally. Sunny felt as if she'd waited a lifetime to be here with him. The taser and mace joined the gun on the floor.

He stood there, unarmed. Sunny bridged the

distance between them, grasped his black T-shirt in both hands and tugged it up his body. She stood on the mattress and he obligingly raised his arms. She tossed the garment on top of his weapons and quickly stripped off his bulletproof vest. She ran her hand over his bare chest. He looked like sculpted perfection but he was all flesh-and-blood male with rock-hard muscles covered in warm, satin skin. His heart thudded beneath her fingertips.

He grasped her hips, holding her in place before him. "Now it's my turn." He worked free the button and zip on her jeans. With exquisite, mind-numbing care he worked the denim over her hips and slid them down her legs. Still standing on the bed, she stepped free of them. Cade wrapped his big hands around her hips, bent his head and nuzzled between her thighs.

Sunny's knees buckled at the wildly erotic sensation of his nose against her satin-covered mound, his lips mouthing her through the material. She held on to his sleekly muscled shoulders. Arousal dampened her panties. She knew he knew just how he affected her and she didn't care. *This* was running free. Together.

"I've wanted you from the moment I saw you on that billboard," she confessed.

He eased her onto the bed, following her down,

his eyes glinting. "And how did you want me?" He cupped her between her legs. "Like this?"

"Yes," she managed to say, stroking the corded muscles of his back.

"Did you imagine my mouth, my tongue, my hands all over you?" He pulled her sweater up and off, leaving her in her bra and panties. He swiped his tongue against her collarbone and she moaned aloud. "Is that how you want me?"

She took him by surprise and pushed him to his back, straddling him midthigh. "Yes. I want to feel your skin against mine." She worked his belt free and then unzipped his pants. She leaned forward and scattered kisses over his six-pack abs. "I want to know your touch, your taste."

With impressive ease, he picked her up and moved her aside. That set her heart to pounding. She was no lightweight and he'd picked her up and moved her off his lap as if she weighed no more than a feather.

"Then it's probably a good idea for me to take off the boots and the pants," he said, sitting up on the side of the bed. He made quick work of it.

He stepped out of his pants and his black briefs and turned to face the bed, his lips parted in a wolfish grin. Sunny's eyes widened at the size of his erection. She'd always thought it was a line of baloney that size didn't matter and it was all in knowing what to do with it. Cade was coming to this party double-armed. He'd definitely been blessed and she was altogether sure he knew precisely how to use it.

He knelt on the edge of the bed, his eyes glittering hot. "I want you naked."

With a slow sensual smile she unhooked her bra and slid it over her arms, down her breasts.

He sucked in a breath and a ravening hunger slammed her at the heat in his eyes. She knew her breasts were small, actually she was more nipple than breast, her areolae were huge, but that suddenly seemed like just the right combination with him and that lean, hungry look.

He wrapped his hands around her waist and leaned her forward. He tongued her pale-pink nipple. Oh. My. God. Sensation rocked her. He rolled her onto her back and took her in his mouth, sucking on her turgid tip and she bucked against him.

He insinuated his leg between hers while he continued to feast on her breasts. One flick of his tongue and she writhed beneath him.

"Beautiful," he murmured as he nuzzled the underside of one soft mound.

"They're small," she said.

"Honey, you're perfect. These perky babies are never going to sag."

She gasped and looked down at him. "I can't believe you actually said that."

"It's a good thing."

He caught her up in his lips and tugged, sucking harder and harder, her hips rising with each movement, her moans punctuating the air. Just when she thought she'd either die from want or actually come, he released her nipple. His breath rasped as harsh as her own.

"Turn around. On your knees."

Recognition and anticipation shivered through her. The way of the wolf.

She knelt on the bed, still wearing her underwear, her buttocks thrust in the air in his direction. He slipped his finger past her underwear and slid it along the edge of her fold. Her world spun. His laugh was low, husky and arrogant. "Oh, honey. You are so hot and so wet. This excites you, doesn't it?" He slid his large finger inside her and a low moan keened in the back of her throat. She pushed herself back against his finger.

"That sounds like a yes to me." He withdrew his finger, grabbed her underwear in both hands and ripped them down the side seam. He pushed them aside and they fell drunkenly around her right thigh.

That was the mother of all turn-ons. He hadn't asked permission, he didn't apologize, he'd just ripped them off. How many times had she fantasized that?

"Sunny—" he murmured behind her. Her muscles clenched in anticipation at the crackle of a cellophane wrapper…

She instinctively spread her knees farther apart and dropped lower, looking over her shoulder and issuing him an age-old invitation.

He'd awakened something primal and instinctive deep within her. It was the call he'd issued the first time she'd seen him on that billboard. He was every inch the dominant male and she was his bitch in heat.

He entered her in one smooth, sure stroke, filling her until she thought she couldn't possibly accommodate all of him. She dropped her shoulders, tilting her hips higher and he drove farther until he was fully sheathed inside her. They both stilled. The connection with him, to him, she'd sensed before she'd ever met him was complete.

He pulsed deep inside her and her muscles grasped him in an instinctive response. She fisted the comforter in her hands, every sense heightened. The scent of him behind her, the exquisite fullness of him inside her, the rightness, the union of more than flesh, the meeting of spirits. He began a slow in-and-out, give-and-take and she met each of his thrust with one of her own.

Wrapping one arm around her, beneath her, he leaned forward and she turned her head to meet him in a kiss. His tongue stroked hers, tangled with her own even as he thrust into her, filled her with his sheathed hardness.

Maybe it was the angle, maybe it was his size, all she knew was that something inside her was being stroked that had never been stroked before, emotionally, mentally, physically. Tension built inside her, winding tighter with each thrust.

She raced with him across a plain of intense, erotic pleasure, filled with a wild exhilaration and an underlying joy that radiated from her core as they began to climb toward a pinnacle. Higher, faster, harder until they reached the top together and the world shattered around her, inside her in a kaleidoscope of fragmented sensation.

Her first coherent thought came to her with a startling clarity. She was marked for life. Regardless of the outcome, regardless of the present or whether it was four weeks or four years or four lifetimes, she was his.

CADE WRAPPED HIS ARMS around Sunny. Lying on their sides, still connected, she nestled against him, her head beneath his chin.

Cade wasn't sure what had just happened. Sex

was not a new game to him. He'd played it many times before but it had never, ever been like what he'd just had with Sunny. It had been like running free and she'd been *with* him, with him in a place inside him no one else had ever visited, had ever known. It had been magical, like sunlight and pleasure and a state of being that he'd never experienced.

Fast on the heels of that realization followed an intense territorial possessiveness. And once again, he'd never felt this way about any of his other lovers. Was it because he'd never invested himself, never moved beyond the motions because he knew in four weeks he'd pack up and move on? Or was it Sunny? He suspected it was both. He had known she'd be complicated. He smiled to himself and pressed a kiss to the top of her hair.

"What?" she murmured, stroking his forearm where it lay against her belly.

"I'm thinking that I knew you were going to be a pain in the ass before I ever met you."

She nipped his shoulder.

"What the hell?" he exclaimed, more surprised than anything.

With the element of surprise working in her favor, in one smooth motion she slid up, disconnecting them, and rolled, sending him flat on his back, leaning over him, pinning him to the mattress. Amusement and challenge danced in her purple eyes. God, she was magnificent. "Funny. I didn't get the impression I was a pain in your ass a few minutes ago."

They both knew he could overpower her in a second. What had started out as light teasing shifted to intense in the span of a heartbeat. He knew he shouldn't ask. He knew it was boorish and bad sex etiquette and all that stuff but he couldn't seem to stop himself. He couldn't abide the thought that another man had felt the same magic with her. "Sunny, has it ever been—"

She cut him off with a finger to his lips. "No. Never with anyone else."

She left it there. Relief flooded him. Not only had she never gone there with anyone else, she didn't need to talk it to death. Halle-effing-lujah! "Good."

She stretched out across his chest, propping herself on one elbow on the other side of the mattress. "I had some great news today. Cecil will probably drop the felony charges."

She gave him a rundown on the sidewalk Santa showing up and the subsequent discussions.

"Cecil will drop them," he said, absently twining a piece of her hair around his finger. "He may stretch it out a day or two to play with your nerves, but it's an opportunity for him to look forgiving." He was, however, damn glad the possibility of her doing jail time would be a moot point.

"He's not one of the good guys," she said. "I'm sure there's something out there on him. I'm not a sore loser. If I thought he'd truly do a good job for the people of Memphis…" He saw it in her eyes. It wasn't about having lost. It truly was a matter of her caring about the city and the people and wanting to make a difference. "I've been nosing around because I'm sure he's not honest."

That clenched his gut, and not in a good way. He cupped her chin in his hand. "The more someone has at stake, the more dangerous they become."

"But—"

"I've got a private detective checking him out. My guy's a professional. It's what he does for a living. And he carries a gun. Let him handle it."

Her eyes widened and then narrowed. "You hired a private detective? When?"

"The day Meeks put out that flyer."

"Why?"

"Because my gut had told me all along that he was bad news. Then when he did that…I thought it was the least I could do."

"Maybe I could share the information I've got so far, which isn't much."

He nodded. "I'll give you his number and you can call him." He traced his hand along her arm and she shivered beneath his fingertips. "Tomorrow."

She smiled and leaned forward to press an openmouthed kiss to his chest. Her hummingbird sat on her shoulder. He captured her hand in his, noticing not for the first time the silver ring on her finger. A hummingbird drinking from a flower. Her hands were broad and capable with long, slender fingers. Her nails were well-kept but blunt and unpolished. He traced his finger against the ring. "So, you're a hummingbird? What does that mean exactly?"

He hoped like hell it didn't mean she went from flower to flower. Not that there was anything very flowerlike about him, but…

"If you're really interested, you should look it up. There're lots of Web sites."

Yeah. It interested him. Obviously it was very important to her since she bore two hummingbird symbols, one permanent. If it was that important to her, then he wanted to know about it.

"I will," he said.

"Maybe you'll figure yours out," she said with a secretive smile that made him want to ask more. But then she slid down his body and swirled her tongue around the base of his shaft, sending an instant wake-up-and-play-again invitation to his dick and he forgot all about anything except for her invite.

12

THE NEXT MORNING Cade dressed for work and watched Sunny lay sprawled, mostly on his side of the bed, dead to the world. She wasn't faking it because it'd be fairly impossible for her to fake that little snoring/sighing thing she did. But then again, he had first-hand experience that Sunny didn't fake anything.

It was…different to wake up to her in his bed, her legs intertwined with his, her hair tickling against his chin, her hogging the covers. He'd never brought a woman to his house over the years. He'd never shared his bed with a woman. He'd always gone to the woman's place or the occasional hotel. It was the same *keep it simple, keep it uncomplicated* theory behind the four weeks.

Sunny issued one of her little snoring sighs. Just as he'd known from the beginning, she was nothing but complication.

The sheet twisted around her, one long leg lay

outside the covers. She was ticklish behind her knee. And when he nuzzled that spot on her hip between her hip and her belly she came unglued. He leaned forward to flick his tongue against that spot and watch her squirm in her sleep but caught himself. If he did, there was no way in hell he was walking out that door. Instead he tugged the comforter over her leg and left the room.

He stopped off in the kitchen and pulled a pen and notepad out of the junk drawer. He wrote a brief note reminding Sunny to take the car if she needed it and giving her Jones's name and number. He hesitated for a moment and then added a line that he'd be back midafternoon—not to account for himself but so she'd be ready. Linc would give him hell for working banker's hours but screw him.

He shrugged into his jacket and closed the back door behind him. He started across the grass. It looked like the forecasted late-afternoon snow would show up. Dense, light-gray clouds blanketed the sky. Snow clouds.

He was almost to the garage door when he caught a movement out of the corner of his eye. He turned his head. At the edge of the woods abutting the meadow stood an animal that looked like a wolf. Shaggy coat, broad chest, watchful eyes. For a second, it was as if the animal looked Cade straight in the eyes. The hair on the back of his neck stood up.

Cade blinked. The wolf was gone. He shook his head and laughed at himself. It must've been a stray dog. Once, years ago, he thought he'd seen a wolf but then he'd done some research. There were no wolves in western Tennessee.

SUNNY OPENED A BOTTLED WATER from the fridge and settled back down on the bar stool, determined to get through her daily to-do list. Classic jazz played on the laptop, courtesy of satellite radio. The house felt happy this morning. Some of the loneliness and melancholy she'd sensed on her arrival had disappeared. What the heck? She felt happy this morning. She glanced at her watch. Well, technically it was now afternoon.

She was amazed that she'd accomplished as much as she had today. She'd had to focus because a night of great, tilt-your-world-on-its-axis sex could be a little distracting the morning after. She'd called Danny Jones, Cade's PI and then gotten a call from her attorney. Meeks had officially dropped the charges.

Sunny picked at the label on the bottled water. As awful as the last month had been, as much as she hated that Meeks was still in office, she wouldn't go back and change any of it if she could. If things had unfolded any differently she wasn't sure that she would've ever met Cade. He might ultimately break her heart if she wasn't careful but for now, he was the silver lining in the past month's thundercloud.

Yearning bloomed low in her belly and spread through her. She ached for him to fill her once again, to feel his weight between her legs, to have his heavy cock buried inside her, his tongue mating with hers, his scent on her skin, his hands pleasuring her breasts. How was it that she was so thoroughly infatuated with him so quickly? She'd never been this way before.

As if the very force of her desire had called to him, she heard the rumble of his car outside. Anticipation flashed through her.

She finished up her e-mail correspondence and closed out of the program. She ran a hand over her hair as a sudden onslaught of self-consciousness flooded her. Yesterday and last night had been wonderful but was it an anomaly? What if…

Her *what if* insecurity was lost to her when her entire body quickened as he stalked across the yard, sure of what he wanted. She sensed the sexual energy radiating from him, and he wasn't even in the house yet.

Her self-consciousness fell to the wayside when he walked in the door. She was out of her chair and met him halfway. He dragged her up hard against the length of his body and she wrapped her arms around his neck. His lips took hers in a kiss that had her straining against him and tangling her tongue with his in an intimate greeting. He followed the curve of her back to cup her bottom in his big hands, kneading, squeezing. She strained against him, aroused by the way he touched her. It was as if he awoke every animalistic, carnal impulse in her, sloughing off all restraints, every civilized nicety she'd ever possessed. He'd issued the call of the wild and she'd responded. She wanted his hand in her pants, stroking her, fondling her.

She made a sound in the back of her throat and he raised his head.

"Um. I like your hello," he drawled. He rubbed his face next to hers, his mouth mere inches from her ear. "Did you sleep in? Did you get some rest?" His low gravel tone scorched her.

"I'm fully rested."

"I brought you something." He reached down and grabbed a bag off the floor that she hadn't even noticed before. He handed her a gift-wrapped box.

Sunny's heart thumped against her ribs. Wasn't

he the man who didn't give gifts? "A present? Did I have a time lapse? It's not even Christmas yet."

"I thought you might want to celebrate Meeks dropping the charges."

"You know?" She paused, holding the bag in her hand.

He shrugged. "I made a few inquiries. It helps to have court and police connections." He nodded toward the bag. "Open it."

She glanced at the wrapping and laughter bubbled up. "I bet you caused quite the stir when you showed up to shop there." *There* was an upscale, slightly risqué boutique. She'd bought a friend a bridal shower gift there once. She didn't want to think about how he knew to shop there. The salesgirls had probably fallen all over themselves to help him. Then again, maybe he hadn't picked it out. "Or did you send Marlene?"

"Uh, no. That would ruin my no-presents reputation and I'm pretty sure she wouldn't like the same thing I like."

"How do you know I'll like it?"

"I don't. But I liked it."

"Typical male."

"Open it. If you don't like it, I'll take it back tomorrow."

She opened the package.

Black lace and mesh panties with a purple bow at the center. Crotchless. A matching black lace bra, with slits in the cups over the nipple area, matching purple bows holding them together. A pair of black lace slippers on four-inch heels completed the outfit.

"Crotchless. Slitted. Heeled. How positively Neanderthal." How positively titillating.

He grinned, that slightly crooked, baby-I'm-going-to-rock-your-world grin. "What about the purple ribbon? I thought it matched your eyes."

"I'm so sure you'll be looking at my eyes." She hoped he wasn't looking at her eyes. If she had her way, his attention would be somewhere else.

"I've got a deal for you. You go put them on and I'll take them off."

SUNNY'D WORN SEXY UNDIES occasionally before but she'd never had a man pick out something specifically for her, something he wanted her to wear expressly for him, and nothing quite so daring. The thought knifed through her that this might be standard procedure for him and she quickly tossed the idea aside. It didn't matter. All that mattered was that he'd bought this for *her* and she wanted to wear it for *him*.

She shimmied out of her clothes and stood

naked for a moment. She did not have a lingerie model's body. She bit her lip and turned to the side, looking at her reflection in the mirror.

Why hadn't she spent more time doing ab work and less time eating? Then she wouldn't have that round little pooch and maybe her butt wouldn't jiggle when she wiggled? But she hadn't and what the hell, most women didn't have a lingerie model figure. What she had was one sexy bad boy waiting on her to come out wearing what he'd brought her.

She pulled on the panties and her self-consciousness fell away. It was a nice fit. She was grateful they weren't thongs. She didn't think she could wear a thong even for him. Well, that wasn't strictly true. If he gave her a thong, she'd wear it, but this was a much sexier, much more flattering cut. Black lace rode midway down her hip and cut to a vee in the center. She turned one way and then the other. She looked pretty damn hot. And she felt very damn hot. There was a lot to be said for the sexy quotient of crotchless underwear.

She slipped on the shoes and immediately felt deliciously, wickedly sexy. Before she put on the bra—because it felt pretty hot to stand around in crotchless panties and hooker heels—she decided to touch up her makeup. More than once in the past two days—had it only been two days?—yep, she'd rammed Cecil on Monday and today was Wednesday—she'd been grateful that she always carried touch-up eye makeup in her purse. Mascara-less was not her idea of her at her best.

This outfit called for a little drama. She heavily outlined her eyes. It was different, exotic. Darker eye shadow in the crease of her lids. She outlined her lips with a lip pencil, having to correct it twice because her hand shook slightly. Yeah, she was nervous, excited, aroused.

She dug in her makeup bag until she found the tube of long-lasting non-smearing lipstick with the wand applicator. Dark mango. She filled in her lips. It even had the faint taste of mango.

She squeezed a dab of hair gel on her hands and leaned over, running her hands through her hair for a messed, wild look. She slowly raised her head and looked in the mirror. She looked like someone else, a foreign, exotic siren. She reached for the bra and she looked from her exotic face to the pale tips of her nipples and she had an idea. She was going for wild, dramatic, exotic.

Nah. She couldn't. She glanced again from her wild mango-darkened lips to her too-demure crests. That would be sort of…erotic. For centuries women in the Far East had adorned themselves with rouges and hennas.

She opened the lipstick and darkened first one nipple, then the other, stimulated by the sight of her rouged breasts. She blotted any excess with a tissue. She hoped Cade didn't have any fruit allergies. Sending him into anaphylactic shock could definitely put a damper on things.

She put on the bra. Another perfect fit. He'd obviously checked her sizes before he left this morning. Smart man.

She was totally, thoroughly turned on just by dressing up for him.

She slipped a finger between her thighs and then dabbed her finger on her wrist and then again along her neck. Sometimes a woman had to make do with what she had available.

Now if she could just make it down the stairs without killing herself in these heels. Tripping wasn't sexy.

TENSION CORDED HIS MUSCLES when he heard her crossing the upstairs landing and he leaned against the door frame of the parlor. Her heels echoed on the wooden treads as she made her way slowly down the stairs.

He'd known she'd be hot in the outfit, but he'd really had no idea just how sexy until she appeared. An instant, ball-busting, suck-all-the-air-out-of-his-lungs inferno swept through him and his dick sprang to immediate, ready-to-serve attention.

He pushed away from the wall and stopped at the bottom of the stairs. Sunny was smokin' hot. She stopped one step from the bottom. With the heels on, she stood at eye level with him.

He opened his mouth but his brain seemed to have shut down and the only thing that came out of his mouth was a cross between a moan, a groan and a grunt.

Sunny wrapped her hand around the back of his neck and leaned in close, nuzzling his jaw. "It fits. Do you like it?"

God, she smelled like sex.

"Fuck me."

"That was the plan," she said with a soft laugh.

He didn't realize he'd spoken aloud until she murmured that against his ear. He hadn't actually meant to say it. It had just popped out, a subconscious exclamation.

She cupped his face in her two hands and kissed him, a slow, sensual journey of her tongue exploring the contours of his mouth. She smelled like sex and tasted like some exotic fruit. He finally gathered enough wits about him to kiss her back.

He ran his hands up the back of her legs to cup her luscious rear in his hands. She uttered a mewling noise into his mouth and sucked on his tongue, which arrowed straight to his crotch.

Her eyes were heavy-lidded with arousal when she broke away from the kiss. "The 'Vette. I want to do it in the car."

"Now? You want to do it in the Corvette?"

"Uh-huh. I've got a thing about sexy muscle cars." Somewhere in the back of his mind, where he could still connect a few functioning brain cells he remembered. "I would really, really like to do it in that car."

He'd been thinking right here on the stairs would work out just fine. "Woman, are you crazy? It's thirty-something degrees outside and the garage isn't heated."

"We could heat it up." She said, her mouth right next to his ear. She smoothed her hands over his chest and nipped his ear lobe, sending a fireball of lust through him. "I promise it'll be hot."

"It'll be tight."

"Tight is best. Tight and hot. How can you turn that down?"

"You want a ride in my 'Vette, then I'll take you for a ride."

13

"THE PASSENGER SEAT is the only way this is going to work," Cade said, so revved up he wasn't even feeling the cold. He stood Sunny on her feet outside the car.

She snuggled into the jacket that he'd thrown around her, which hit her midthigh, and smiled. "That's fine by me."

He opened the passenger door and climbed in the car. He'd thought she was sort of crazy, but now he was thinking it was a pretty hot idea. Some parts of him were thinking it was a very hot idea. He patted his lap. "Climb on in, baby and I'll take you for a ride."

"This is so hot," she said and climbed in on top of him, which was no small feat of maneuvering. Finally, she was astride his lap and he pulled the car door closed.

This was a very good position. Her open thighs nestled against the hard ridge of his erection. Even through his pants he could feel her heat, feel her juicy mound against him.

She let the front of his jacket fall open, but kept it around her shoulders. She reached down and tugged his T-shirt free from his waistband, sliding her hands beneath the material. She explored the ridges of his muscles, her touch affecting him like an aphrodisiac. "Can you take off the shirt?"

He pulled it over his head and tossed it into the other seat. She offered a satisfied sigh and cast an appreciative, incendiary glance at his bare chest. "You have the most gorgeous body," she said, her voice a low, seductive purr. "Sexy guy. Sexy car. It works."

He stroked his hands up the outside of her legs. "It definitely works for me." Her skin was like a soft chamois cloth. "So, how long have you had a thing for muscle cars?" He cupped his hands around her hips.

"I've always found them—" she shifted her sex against his "—exciting."

He caressed the tops of her thighs with his thumbs. "And how about the guys that drive them?"

"Hmm. I'll have to think about that for a while."

His jacket joined his T-shirt in the other seat.

"Maybe I can help you make up your mind," he said. He reached behind her, between her nicely rounded cheeks, and found the opening in her panties. He slid his finger farther into her drenched curls. She dropped her head onto his chest and made a soft mewling sound in the back of her throat. She shifted farther up onto her knees, allowing him access. He slipped a finger inside her silky hot channel. She gasped and lightly bit his bicep. He added another finger and she clenched around him. "What is it you like about muscle cars?"

"Muscle cars are sexy—" she fingered his flat, male nipples and pleasure arrowed all the way through him, tightening his balls "—raw—" she rocked back on his fingers "—with a little bit of a rough edge." He slowly pulled his fingers almost all the way out and then slid them back into her, loving the way she bit down on her lip and threw her head back. The way she clenched around him. "I'm partial to a big block engine with a manual overdrive." He found her button with another finger and she was panting. "I like—" she reached between them "—driving with my hand—" she grasped him through his pants "—on the gear shift."

He kept a slow measured rhythm. "You find that exciting?"

"Immensely." She canted back, taking him deeper, a small moan escaping. "What is it you like about driving this car?"

"She's unpredictable and temperamental. You've got to know just the right way to handle her—" he withdrew his fingers and she whimpered a protest "—but once you figure that out—" he brushed his finger, glistening with her essence, over her lower lip "—she's responsive." She captured his wrist in her hand. She swirled her tongue around his finger and then took it in her mouth, sucking on it. First one finger, then the other. He groaned aloud and she uttered her pleasure in the back of her throat. "The harder and faster you drive her, the better she handles," he managed to say.

She leaned into him and kissed him, letting him taste her. He suckled her lower lip. "Delicious," he murmured against her mouth.

"You like driving hard and fast?" she asked. She scooted back far enough to lean down and swipe her tongue against his nipple.

"It depends on the mood. There's a lot to be said for taking it slow and easy." He splayed his hands across her back and tugged her to him. He kissed her, a slow measured exploration that absorbed every sensation of her sprawled against his chest in the close confines of the car. Her heart thudded against his chest. He slanted his head and showered kisses along her neck, feeling her quiver against him as he nuzzled the juncture of her shoulder and neck.

She smoothed her hands over his chest, stroking, kneading, her fingers exploring him, as if she wanted to memorize every inch of his chest, shoulders and arms.

He really, really wanted to untie those purple ribbons on the front of her bra with his teeth. Given the fact that his head was damn near brushing the roof and there wasn't much room for him to lean forward with her on his lap—not that he was complaining—he contented himself with untying the bows with his fingers. A secretive smile danced around her mouth.

He tugged one end, pulling the ribbon across her nipple and she shuddered. "That feels good?"

"You have no idea." Her voice was low, breathy, sexy.

He drew both ribbons at the same time and she arched her back and came up on her knees, banging her head against the roof.

That was not the intended outcome. "You okay?" he asked.

She laughed and rubbed the top of her head with one of her hands. "I'm fine. It just felt so good—" she wiggled in his lap "—when you pulled the ribbon out, not when I banged my head."

Sunny lost him on the very last part. His attention had been caught and held by her very dark tips peeking out at him through the front openings. She didn't have dark nipples. Hers were a pale pink that flushed to a light rose when he kissed them. These were much darker.

"See something you like?" she asked with a faux innocence.

"Are they—"

"They are." She cupped her breasts in her hands and squeezed, sending them farther through the openings. "Lipstick. Mango flavored. What do you think?"

She leaned forward, offering him a darkened peak. He drew her into his mouth and sucked the mango flavor off her sweet nipple. "Harder," she said, panting, grinding down against his throbbing cock. He licked and sucked both of her breasts until he thought he'd come without ever being inside her. And he very much wanted inside her.

He wanted her with the wild abandon of a horny teenager in the back seat of a car. His chest was heaving when he leaned his head back on the headrest. "I think you are one sexy woman. I think I want to be inside you. Now."

He unzipped his pants and together he and Sunny shoved them, along with his underwear down to his knees. They fumbled over one another, rushing to roll a condom over his swollen cock. Finally it was on.

She grasped his shoulders and levered herself up over his eager, aching, rock-hard, take-me-inside-you-now dick. He grasped her hips as she slowly sank down onto him. He gritted his teeth. She was so dripping, drowning slick, hot, wet and so damn tight he thought he might actually die.

She stopped and he tried to pull her further down but she had the leverage and pushed back up until he was back out of her. She eased down again, just sheathing the top of his cock in her. He tried thrusting up but with the angle of the seat, his pants bunched around his knees and he couldn't go far.

"Sunny," he growled.

She leaned into his shoulder because otherwise she'd hit the roof. This time she slid a little farther down on him, but then slowly, excruciatingly slid right back up.

"Focus," she said, her voice breathy against his shoulder, "on how good it feels *now.* Close your eyes and let yourself feel it. Feel how wet you make me. How hot I am for your beautiful thick cock." She took more of him on the downslide. Jesus, she felt so good and he loved her sexy talk.

Fever gripped him. The world, his existence distilled to this—her slow ride astride him, the snug silken heat of her channel stroking up and down his cock, the warm lap of her juices against him. She held the key. Only she could satiate him. Only she could give him what he wanted, what he craved, what he needed.

When he didn't think he could stand any more, when he wanted to howl with the need to be buried inside her, she took all of him. He clamped her hips in place and she rocked against him, inching him deeper, more fully inside her.

She moaned and he answered her with his own. She fused her mouth to his and their tongues mimicked their bodies. He shifted his hips and thrust. Now. With him filling her, it was enough to feel her muscles tighten and pulse around him.

Together they shifted into overdrive. She let him set the rhythm as he guided her up and down, faster, harder, her bottom slapping against his thighs. He swallowed all the sexy sounds she made into his mouth. He felt her muscles clench harder as she pistoned faster, her cries becoming more harsh, urgent, her nails scoring his shoulders. She was about to climax and he was ready to explode. Ladies first. He reached between her thighs and found her clit, massaging her pearl.

At the first onslaught of her orgasm he joined her. Sensation ripped him, pleasure so intense it bordered on pain roared through him, carried him beyond reason to some elemental, fundamental part of his being.

Panting against his throat, Sunny licked a lazy path from his neck to his ear and nipped him. "That was some ride."

LATER, AFTER A MUCH-NEEDED SHOWER, which had taken a detour when Cade offered to wash her back and had wound up washing other parts in a very intimate, thorough manner, Sunny sat at the kitchen counter, wearing one of his sweatshirts, and watched him cook dinner. He'd slipped on a pair of gray sweatpants that rode low on his hips, a worn Tennessee Vols T-shirt hugged his broad shoulders. Desire, always simmering around him, flared inside her. You'd think she'd be spent from earlier, but with him around… She sipped at a glass of buttery chardonnay.

She traced her finger along the glass stem and broached the subject of tomorrow. "I need to go home tomorrow. Could you give me a lift on your way in?"

He paused briefly, putting the asparagus in the steamer, his expression unreadable. "Don't feel like you have to."

"I think I should. I need to get back to my house."

Funny but she really hadn't missed it at all, which was somewhat disconcerting considering it was her space filled with her things. "I've got a stained-glass piece I'm working on that I'm itching to get back to." That much was at least true. She wanted to finish the wolf piece she'd started. And she knew exactly where it belonged. The *where* was a bank of windows that ran across the back of the dining room, overlooking the meadow beyond. The wolf needed to stand sentinel the same as Cade stood sentinel over the house and his family. And her.

It would be so easy to stay here. This was like being wrapped in a cocoon where the rest of the real world only temporarily intruded. Where Cade cushioned the outside and only bits and pieces filtered through. She could hang out in this fabulous house and do her Web work via the Internet while he cooked and brought her presents and they had glorious sex and bit by bit, she feared, she'd lose her identity to him. She felt herself inextricably intertwined with him, but she also felt a need to set herself apart. He was the type of man a woman could lose herself in.

He nodded and leaned against the counter. "I can give you a ride or you can take the beater until you get your car back. It just sits in the garage."

"That's nice but it could be a while before I get

my car back. I…uh, did a good bit of damage to the front end. Unfortunately I've got lawyer fees to cover and I sunk a lot of money, well, for me it was a lot of money, into my campaign fund."

"Send your car out here. I'll take care of the body work."

"But—"

"Sunny, it's what I do in my spare time. It relaxes me and I'm good at it."

She laughed because she certainly knew one thing that relaxed him and he was damn good at. He leaned across the counter and stole a kiss. "I think you have a dirty mind." He grinned. "A most admirable trait. We could work out a trade."

"I don't know what the going rate is for a front-end replacement."

He raked her with a simmering look. "I'm sure you can cover the costs."

"Okay." Sunny let it go. If he wanted to do it. She just wasn't used to anyone stepping in to help.

Cade finished up dinner. She loved watching him in the kitchen. Was there anything sexier than a gorgeous caveman in the kitchen? Well, duh. A gorgeous caveman in a Corvette. A shiver slid down her spine just thinking about earlier.

Tomorrow morning she was going home. She eyed the cushions still piled in the sunroom.

"Want to picnic? There on the floor?"

"Sure, why not? You want to eat on the floor, we'll eat on the floor." He brushed her cheek with the back of his hand.

Something warm and fragile bloomed inside her. He was such a contradiction, so much more complex than she'd thought he'd be when she tagged him a caveman. She thought it was sweet that he'd so willingly indulge her whim.

"Do you have a candle?" she asked.

"No candles. But I have an oil lamp I keep around for when the electricity goes out."

"Perfect."

Within a minute or so he'd lit the lamp and placed it on the floor and brought dinner over on two plates—salmon, fresh asparagus and a wild mushroom risotto. Sunny carried over the silverware, napkins and wineglasses. They each claimed a cushion, beside each other, but facing one another. Sunny sat Indian style while Cade stretched out his legs.

They lapsed into a companionable silence. Sunny was suddenly starving. Great sex worked up an appetite. The fish was moist and flaky, the asparagus tender but still firm, the risotto delicately seasoned. "Do you eat like this all the time?" she asked.

"Pretty much. I learned to cook when...I was

teenager." She was dead certain he'd almost said something else and caught himself at the last minute. She was equally certain it was about the time his mother died and his father fell apart. "And I figured if I was going to cook, it might as well be decent because I like to eat good food."

"Is there anything you don't do well?" she said, teasing him. She'd felt the shift in him, the banked pain when he mentioned learning to cook.

"There's lots of things I'm not good at. Pretty speeches, pretty phrases." He'd taken her seriously. "I'm not the most sensitive guy. I'm used to having my own way. I can't dance. My brother and sister are a lot of fun. I'm just the guy who shows up every day and gets it done."

He shouldn't shortchange himself. "You've sort of had to be, haven't you?"

He shook his head and speared his asparagus. "Gracie."

"She mentioned a couple of things."

"I know my sister. She gave you way more personal information than you ever wanted to know."

"I didn't ask...but I did want to know." Sunny pushed a mushroom around on her plate. She didn't know what the hell they exactly were. Lovers? Boyfriend/girlfriend? Friends? Her bail bondsman who'd given her some awesome orgasms in the past two days? Well, technically a couple of months if you counted fantasy time and gave him credit for the role he'd played there. "She invited me to the Christmas party Friday night."

"Do you want to come?"

"You know, caveman, you were dead-on with that pretty speeches thing." She elbowed his leg. "A little enthusiasm on your part would be appreciated."

"Do you want to come or not?"

"Am I coming as your sister's invite or as your date?" She felt like upending her wine over his dense head. She shouldn't have to ask.

"How about both? Marlene will be beside herself."

"What about you? Will you be beside yourself?"

"Honey, I've been beside myself since the first time I saw that flyer. I knew before I ever met you, you'd be a pain in my ass."

"Be still my beating heart." Actually, it was pounding like a runaway train. She sniffed. "I knew the minute I saw you on that billboard you'd be a Neanderthal." She swirled her wine in her glass. "I'll check my calendar and make sure I don't have another date that night."

"You can cancel it." His tawny eyes held hers. "We cavemen don't share."

While they were clarifying… "Neither do we

PITAs—that'd be Pain In The Ass to you." She smiled sweetly. "I think I'd like to meet everyone. Marlene who has you whipped, your dad, Linc the artist and guitarist—"

"You can also meet Georgia, Linc's fiancée," he interrupted her with a possessive scowl.

"The wedding planner."

"Did Gracie manage to leave any stone unturned?"

"Hey, be careful. That almost had a poetic ring to it. And I have no idea. How would I know if a stone was unturned?"

"In case she didn't cover it, there's something you should know…."

"The men in your family like to cross-dress for a party?"

"I'll let you take that up with Martin when you meet him. That ad campaign we did with Meeks…I told you we were in a financial crunch, but, for what it's worth, we all voted for you," Cade said.

"That's worth—" She had to clear her throat and start again because it choked her up. "That's worth quite a lot."

Sunny's cell phone rang. She checked the caller ID. She'd given Nadine her new number yesterday. She wasn't up for Nadine. Not now. "It's my sister. She can leave a message."

"Does she always treat you like shit or was she just having a bad day the other day?"

She didn't bother to pretend she didn't know what Cade meant. "Nadine doesn't come across well."

She thought he muttered something along the lines of *damn straight* under his breath.

"She runs around with her glass half empty but you can't really blame her. She's just like my parents."

"Why do you put up with it? Tell her to kiss your ass."

"Nadine's unhappy with herself and it comes through in the way she relates to me."

"But you're so strong otherwise...."

Her heart flip-flopped at his offhand compliment. She found herself telling him about her family and Mrs. Pearl but she wasn't sure if he got it. "We're not close like your family is. We never will be, but she's still my family. I love her despite her faults. Forgiving her, accepting her for who she is, warts and all, doesn't make me weak." A movement outside caught her eye. "Cade, look." He had his back to the window. "Outside. It's snowing."

He looked over his shoulder. Outside the glass, snow drifted down, big fat flakes that floated lazily past them.

He turned back to face her, his expression uncharacteristically tentative.

"When Linc and I were kids, sometimes we'd camp out here. We could do that tonight. If I stoke the fire just right, it should burn for hours. Most of the night."

Camping out on the floor while the snow fell outside around them struck her as wildly romantic. "That would be lovely."

If she wasn't careful she just might find herself in love.

He smiled his sexy, endearing, lopsided smile, his eyes crinkling at the corners and she glimpsed the boy who'd grown into the man.

Careful had come too late.

Cade Stone owned her heart.

"THAT SHOULD LAST FOR A WHILE," Cade said as the fire crackled and popped. He stood, brushing off the dirt clinging to his hands.

"Mmm. Nice. I've got us set up over here."

She'd built a cozy little den of sofa cushions, pillows and comforters in the sunroom. She'd extinguished the oil lamp.

He crossed the room and she pulled back the edge of the comforter, silently inviting him in. He lay down beside her and rolled to his side, propping on his elbow. She spooned against him, her bare legs twining with his, her buttocks snugged against his crotch, her shoulders next to his chest. Her hair tickled his throat.

He'd known she was a pain in the ass before he ever met her. She'd scattered stuff around his house. He'd had to carry her out to the garage. Pull the comforters off the beds upstairs.

And he had a feeling he was going to miss her like hell when she went home tomorrow. She'd brought vibrancy, a new dimension to his life in the last few days.

Unfortunately, he'd spoken the truth earlier. He wasn't a man to turn a pretty phrase. And he wasn't so good at tender, but he'd aim for both.

He curved his arm around her waist. "You look nice in the dark."

She made a strangled sound and rolled to her back to look up at him. "Did you just say I looked nice in the dark? That means I only look good if you can't see me?"

"No." He'd give it another go. "It means I like the way the moonbeams brush your face." Holy shit, had that just really come out of his mouth? He sounded like one of those metrosexuals. Next he'd be signing up to do an underwear ad.

"Cade—"

"Yeah?"

"I think you're more a man of action than words. You know, you're really good with the doing part. You might want to stick with that."

He was much better with the doing. And he hadn't forgotten for a second that she wasn't wearing anything beneath his sweatshirt. He slid his hand up her thigh and she sighed.

He stroked the soft skin of her belly and kissed the side of her neck. "Show, don't tell?"

"Yes." She twined her arms around his neck.

He loved those little breathy one-syllable responses she gave.

"Can I say one more thing? It would really help with the showing business."

"Okay?"

"I sure would like to see you naked in the moonlight."

"Why didn't you say so earlier?" She pulled his sweatshirt over her head in one swift motion. For a moment he was rendered speechless, awe-struck. The moonlight washed parts of her to an alabaster white, while casting other parts in shadow.

He felt as if he'd taken a roundhouse kick to the solar plexus. "You look like a goddess."

Her breath audibly hitched in her throat. "You know, you're getting better at the telling. Maybe you just need to practice."

Her soft laughter turned to a sigh as he threaded his fingers through her hair and proceeded to practice both showing and telling.

14

SUNNY BREATHED A SIGH OF RELIEF and closed her front door behind her. No one had accosted her with a camera on her way in, which was a very good thing. Hopefully everyone had moved on to something far more important. Forget global warming and human rights violations. Maybe a supermodel had sprouted a pimple right before a runway show or another Hollywood starlet had checked herself into rehab. The things people deemed important never ceased to amaze her.

Thursday midafternoon. She'd left with Cade on Monday night. Two and a half days. It felt more like a lifetime.

The small table-top fountain in the foyer burbled a welcome but her house didn't feel nearly as welcoming, as comfortable to her soul as Cade's. She'd always been the odd one out growing up, never fitting in. She'd waited, searched for a place that felt like home. That was what she'd wanted when she'd bought this house. But she knew now that was what she'd found when she'd walked into Cade's house. Home. A place that engendered contentment, belonging.

She climbed the stairs to the third floor to her studio. Sunlight poured in through the rear window, illuminating the various stained-glass pieces she'd hung randomly from the ceiling.

She found a comfort in the familiarity of the rows of glass standing in their crates against two walls, the glass cutter, grinder, pliers, soldering iron and lead came. She stood at the big table placed to catch the window's light where she assembled the glass, where she used woodstrips and horseshoe nails to hold the glass pieces in place until the design was complete and she was ready to solder the lead channel.

Her wolf, Cade incarnate, lay on the table, nearly complete. Yes, those were his eyes, that was the tilt of his head, the faint curl of the lip belonged to him. It was so obvious to her now.

She pushed up the sleeves of her sweater. She had a ton of stuff to do, check her e-mail, sort through her snail mail, grocery shopping, change into something other than these jeans and sweater and drag out her Christmas decorations, but those things could all wait. She was itching to work on her wolf.

She'd just gotten into the rhythm of working when the doorbell rang.

She thought about ignoring it. Another insistent ring and she threw up her hands. Okay. Fine. Maybe the media already had wind of this latest turn of events. If it was a photographer she'd head back upstairs—and yank the wire on the doorbell along the way.

She ran down the last set of stairs and peered through the peephole. Cade. Her heart seemed to do a slow somersault in her chest.

She slid the bolt, released the chain and opened the door.

"Hi." She sounded as breathless as she felt.

It didn't feel as if she'd last seen him five hours ago. It felt closer to an eternity. He stepped inside and seemed to fill her foyer. He tended to have that effect on space. He was a big man with an even bigger presence.

"Hello." He wrapped one arm around her and pulled her against the hard wall of…him. She splayed one hand against his chest, feeling the thud of his heart beneath her fingertips. His mouth descended on hers in a thorough kiss.

Her knees weren't quite steady when the kiss ended and neither was her laugh. "Wow. I'm glad you stopped by."

"I brought lunch. Sandwiches." He hoisted a bag from the deli around the corner. "I thought I'd better make sure you got my car here without ramming anyone."

"Very funny." She wrinkled her nose at him. "The bounty hunter comedian."

"I'm a regular riot act." A frown wrinkled his brow. "Any trouble when you got home?"

Ever the protector. "None." She eyed him from head to toe, thoroughly appreciating the badass bounty hunter black-on-black "uniform." One kiss and he had her sizzling. "I see you managed another morning without getting killed."

"I did. Although you wouldn't be inconvenienced now."

"Shows how little you know. I'd be seriously inconvenienced." She looked him over deliberately, suggestively, letting her gaze linger on the burgeoning bulge in the front of his pants. "You've got something I want."

He smirked. "Is that a fact, Ms. Templeton?"

"That's a fact, Mr. Stone. If you met with an unfortunate end—" she plucked the bag out of his hand "—who would bring me lunch?" She grinned at him. "Most inconvenient."

"Do you have any picnic spots in your house?"

"It's not as nice as your greenhouse but I've got a good spot. Come on." She grabbed his hand in hers and tugged him toward the stairs. "It's up here and I want to show you something."

"You've definitely got something I'd like to see," he said with a leer, eyeing her butt. A thrill ran through her, notching up her internal thermostat.

"Yeah? Well, there's something else you need to see…first." They'd get to *that* later.

She led him up to her studio. Dust motes danced through the sun slanting in the rear window.

Sunny spent a few minutes explaining the design process and showing him the various components. Cade seemed genuinely interested, asking intelligent questions. Sunny knew a thrill of pride that he seemed very impressed that she'd created the pieces hanging.

"But this is what I really wanted to show you," she said, leading him to her assembly table.

She stepped aside and watched him, curious as to his reaction. Would he really *see* it?

Cade looked at the piece and started in surprise. "It's a wolf?"

"Yeah.

He shook his head as if to clear it and gave a funny laugh. "That's strange." He looked at her, a faint perplexity shadowing his face. "Yesterday morning, when I left for work, I thought I saw a wolf at the edge of the woods, but it had to have been a stray dog because there haven't been wolves here in over thirty years."

Sunny smiled. "I started this project a couple of months ago. It was a good stress release during the election." She circled to the other side of him. "Does anything about it look familiar to you?"

He cocked his head to one side and studied it, narrowing his eyes. "It does. I'm good with faces. I have to be in my business." He canted his head to the other side. "But I can't quite nail this one." He shrugged and looked to her.

"It'll come to you." And it would, when he was ready to figure it out. It was all part of his journey. It would speak to him, he'd recognize himself, when he was ready to listen. "It took me a while to figure it out and I'm the artist." Now it was time to show him the something else. "Unless you're starving for lunch, there is something else I think you might be interested in." She grabbed her sweater in both hands, pulled it up and off in one fluid motion, and dropped it to the floor.

"I'm starving," he said with a wicked gleam in his eyes, "but it's not for lunch." He hooked his finger beneath her bra and tugged her to him. "*This* is exactly what I'm craving."

CADE LAY SPRAWLED on her bed, wearing nothing but a satisfied smile on his face. The heady scent of sex, very good sex, hung in the air like an erotic perfume. "Honey, I love your lunchtime menu." He folded his hands behind his head, all masculine arrogance. "Hot. Juicy. Satisfying. I could have that every day."

They'd just made love but Sunny found her body quickening again. She loved it when he said stuff like that. It made her…well, hot. Again.

She knew exactly what she wanted. "I could go for hot and juicy myself," she said, eyeing his naked body. "That is, if your kitchen's not closed."

His sac hung heavy beneath his penis. She knew exactly what she wanted. And thank goodness they'd gotten the awkward bill-of-clean-health part out of the way the other night.

She dipped her head and swirled her tongue over his balls.

"My kitchen's definitely open," he rasped on an indrawn breath.

Wrapping her lips carefully over her teeth she sucked on first one ball and then the other, feeling them tighten in her mouth.

A shudder racked his huge body. She played with him, lapping and sucking until his breath came in hard, short pants. She loved the taste of him in her mouth, the smoothness of him against her tongue, the heady smell of male arousal.

"You're killing me," he gasped. "Put your lips..."

She cupped his testicles in one hand and swirled her tongue around the base of his shaft. "I love the way you feel." She drew her tongue up the length of him and probed her tip along his slitted opening. "The way you taste."

"Sunny..." he rasped.

He seemed incapable of saying more. Good. And it was no hardship. His cock had her wet and hungry. She tongued him like a melting ice cream on a hot day. When she'd worked her way around his world, she rose up over him, taking as much of him in her mouth as possible, reveling in the feel of his gorgeous hard erection. She wrapped her other hand around his base and moved her hand up and down in rhythm with her mouth.

"Oh, honey..." he moaned.

She moved her tongue in circles around his penis while she continued the up-and-down motion. He quivered and the juices of her own excitement flooded her. She wanted more of him. It would be impossible at this angle.

She released him from her mouth and slid up the hard plane of his body, blazing the trail with hot, openmouthed, sucking kisses, until she reached his lips.

"I want all of you," she whispered into his ear, pressing her wet folds against his hip, letting him feel how much sucking him had turned her on.

Sunny rolled to her back, dropping her head over the opposite side of the bed.

He stood, his tawny eyes glowing. He knew exactly what she wanted. He rounded the bed and stood behind her and she wrapped her hands around his hips, her fingers digging into the muscles of his tight ass, pulling him forward, taking him into her mouth. She dropped her head farther back and drew him deeper.

Delicious. Hot. Erotic. He began to thrust in and out of her mouth. He leaned forward and she felt his mouth between her thighs, his tongue delving between her folds. He found her clit, laving, sucking, even as he rode his cock in and out of her mouth. It was the ultimate sixty-nine position. Cade gasped her name and she tasted him against her tongue as her own orgasm spiraled out of control.

CADE WASN'T TOO DAMN SURE he could move. "Are you trying to kill me?"

"Hmm. You weren't complaining two minutes

ago." She laughed sexily. "At least that didn't sound like a complaint."

His cell phone rang and he leaned over the side of the bed and snagged it from his pants. "It's Gracie," he said to Sunny. Most of the time when Gracie called it wasn't important but he never knew so he always took the call if he could.

Sunny slid off the bed and padded into the other room, obviously giving him privacy.

"Hey, are you busy?" Gracie asked.

"I'm not in the middle of anything but this better be good."

Gracie laughed on the other end. "It's better than good. I just ran by the office and you are not going to believe it." She paused for dramatic effect. "Daddy and Marlene are going on a cruise."

"Yeah? So? He likes to gamble and he likes to dance. She must, too."

"In February. As in two months from now. Two months being *eight* weeks. Do you get it?"

"Yeah. I get it." He'd have to be simple not to. Martin, the original architect of the four-week rule of dating, was making plans eight weeks out with Marlene? Hell had just frozen over. And he'd warned Martin not to hurt Marlene but now…what was he thinking?

"I think he's afraid someone else is gonna snatch her up," Gracie said.

Sunny padded back into the bedroom, unfortunately no longer naked, and Cade knew *exactly* what Gracie meant. How in the hell had he ever thought his four-week rule would work with Sunny? Because he'd never felt this way with any other woman. Connected. As if he'd found something he never even knew he was looking for. He liked her, admired her, respected her, and he sure as hell didn't want someone else *snatching her up.*

"Are you still there?" Gracie asked, snapping him out of his reverie.

"Yeah. But I've got to go." He hung up.

"Everything okay?" Sunny asked.

He pulled her back to the mattress beside him. "It is now."

The only person snatching her up would be him.

SHE'D JUST TACKED another wood strip into place when her cell phone rang. She glanced at caller ID. Celia, her attorney. Please, don't let Cecil have changed his mind. Could he change his mind? There was only one way to find out. She answered the call.

"Sunny, it's Celia. I have some very, very good news. You might want to sit down."

She sank to the floor, as much from relief that

Cecil hadn't reneged as in anticipation of the impending good news. "I'm sitting."

"How do you feel about taking on the city council seat?"

Sunny's head swam. She was glad of the hardwood beneath her. "What? How? When?"

"It may be several weeks or a couple of months, but that city council seat is yours. Cecil fixed the election."

"He what?"

"Does the name Lavigne Carmidy mean anything to you?"

"No. Should it?"

"Not really. Lavigne was a ballot official in last month's election. Cecil offered her a handsome cash deposit and she conveniently, for him, didn't turn in several boxes of ballots in your favor."

Sunny could hardly breathe, hardly dared to believe it. "And you know this how?"

"Lavigne started feeling guilty when you got such a bad media rap. Then when all this came down with the wreck, she snapped. She went to the district attorney this morning and turned herself in."

"But won't it be her word against his?"

"Lavigne took out an insurance policy. She knew if it ever came down to it, Cecil would hang her out to dry. He paid her in small denominations of unmarked bills. She, however, secretly tape-recorded their conversation when she played dumb and he spelled out for her exactly how she was to take the ballots and then dispose of them. Her plan was to blackmail him for more money down the road."

"Oh, my God."

"Exactly. Lavigne was watching a revival on late-night TV last night when her conscience smote her and she said God directed her to turn herself in this morning. She did, just as soon as she finished getting a wash and set at the beauty parlor. She said she wanted to look good for the cameras."

"I don't know what to say...."

"Judging from the number of ballots they recovered from Lavigne's garage, you actually won the election. It'll have to move through the legal channels, but sometime in the upcoming year, you'll be sitting our city council seat. Congratulations."

She and Celia wrapped up the conversation and Sunny was ashamed that the first person she thought about telling her news was Cade. Sheila, she admonished herself, should be her first call. She called Sheila and left a brief message outlining the situation on her voice mail. She was still sitting in the studio, a little dazed, when the doorbell rang.

She raced downstairs. She had an inkling it

might be Cade. It was. She closed the door behind him, her heart beginning to sing because he was here and she could share her news with him. "I have some news."

He grinned. "Cecil fixing the election returns?"

"How did you know?"

"I just found out. I thought I'd swing by and make sure you'd heard. Are you excited?"

"I think I'm still processing that it's real," she said. He caught her up in a hug and twirled her around.

She was laughing when he put her back down but she held on to him, her arms wrapped around his waist. He'd known when Cecil was dropping the charges and he'd obviously heard this news before it even made it to her. The man was well connected. She leaned back and looked up into his rugged face. "Do you *always* hear my news before I do?"

"Not always." He paused, a sly humor lighting his eyes. "You had me on the arrest thing." He pressed a kiss to her forehead. "Congratulations, honey. You've got what you wanted and you're going to be the best damn city councilman this city's ever had. It's a damn shame you had to go through the last month to get here."

"I don't regret a minute of it. I'd do it all over again because it brought us together. I love you."

She hadn't planned to say it, it had just bubbled out in a moment of spontaneous oral combustion. And now that it was said, she was glad she had. When you loved someone you needed to tell them. Love was a joy that deserved sharing.

Cade pulled her close again and kissed her. It did not, however, escape her notice that he didn't comment on her declaration of love. She was pretty sure that didn't portend well.

She was perceptive that way.

A WEEK AND A HALF LATER the AA Atco Christmas party was in full swing. Cade watched Sunny, Marlene, Georgia and Gracie sitting around the dining room table talking and laughing as if they were all old friends. Sunny had fit right in, charming them all. He'd known she would.

She was talking now, her face animated, her hands punctuating her comments. Even in the middle of the party a familiar current of attraction surged through him. There was a pause as all the women looked at him and then burst into laughter. God knows what she was telling them.

"Don't believe a word she says," he called out over the jazz Christmas CD playing in the background, "she's a pathological liar."

"Right, caveman," Georgia, Linc's fiancée,

yelled back at him, sending all the women into another laughing fit.

Cade turned to Linc propping up the counter in the kitchen with him, each of them nursing a beer. "Can't you do something with that woman of yours?"

Linc grinned, shaking his head. "Georgia is a law unto herself. Same as your woman."

Sunny was his woman. And Sunny was definitely her own person. "That's for damn sure."

"It's different with her, isn't it? Than all the others?"

Sunny, and his relationship with her, was outside the realm of anything else he'd ever experienced. She was not only his lover, but they'd developed a friendship. He knew she loved him and he…cared for her.

"Yeah. She's a pain in my ass." When he looked back on it, his life had been damn boring before her.

"You might as well give it up, Cade." Linc's look was part sympathetic, part congratulatory. "Don't you remember what a monumental pain Georgia was?"

The CD changed tracks during the last of his declaration, leaving it echoing across the room. Georgia skewed Linc with a look. "You were saying, darling?"

"Just reaffirming how much I adore you."

"That's what I thought." Georgia smiled and returned to the conversation.

He and Linc spent a few minutes discussing how Sunny's Mustang was coming along and a couple of FTAs. Gracie came into the kitchen and poured herself a cup of coffee. His sister was the last person in need of caffeine.

"No shoptalk allowed. Hel-lo. It's a party," she said.

"Tell that to Mark." Cade nodded at his future brother-in-law outside. "That boy needs to grow some balls."

Martin had bullied Mark into going outside for a game of horseshoes. They were playing with the floodlight turned on. It was only thirty-something friggin' degrees outside. And Martin was probably cheating to boot.

"Mark likes Daddy," she said. "That's why he humors him. It is not a lack of cojones, caveman."

"I'm going to have to separate you and Sunny." God, he'd known his sister and Sunny would be trouble together. And throw Georgia and Marlene into the mix, too. None of the men in this family would ever know a moment of peace.

"She's a keeper," Gracie said.

"Thank you for that insight," he offered dryly.

"Welcome." Her smile was positively smug

when she pranced out of the kitchen. Sarcasm was often wasted on his sister.

Linc quirked an eyebrow. “Is she a keeper?”

Sunny was one of a kind. They were compatible. She needed him to take care of her. They belonged together.

“Yeah. She is.”

And he knew just what he was getting her for Christmas.

15

"MERRY CHRISTMAS," Sunny said, passing her gift to Cade very carefully since it was big and awkward. Wrapping it had been a challenge.

An expectant hush settled around the table, his entire family quieting, which in and of itself was amazing. Wrapping paper littered the floor all around them. She and Cade, at his request, were the last to exchange gifts around the long table.

He began to smile before he even had all of the paper off. "Sunny made this," he told his family as he finished unwrapping it.

He held up the wolf stained glass for everyone to see. There were lots of exclamations but it was Gracie, not surprisingly, who noticed first.

"Oh, wow! How'd you do that?" she asked Sunny. "It's a wolf, but it looks just like Cade."

"It's the eyes," Marlene said.

"It's the same way he tilts his head," Georgia observed.

Cade looked down at the big piece of stained glass he held in his hands and Sunny saw the light-bulb go off. "It's me."

"It's you," she said. "The protector. The guardian."

"That's perfect!" Gracie said.

"How'd you do it so fast?" Linc asked with a frown. It would take another artist to realize how much time would be involved.

"I started it a couple of months ago. After the billboards went up but I didn't realize it was Cade until the night he bailed me out of jail." She looked at him tenderly, uncaring that she was baring her soul in front of his entire family. "The wolf standing between me and the world."

"Thank you," Cade said, bending to kiss her. Her heart turned over at his gentleness. He straightened and handed her a gift-wrapped box. "You said you wanted something expensive," he reminded her with a grin.

If it was anything of a sexual nature he'd just handed her to open in front of his family, he was one dead man. It was big but it wasn't very heavy. She tore through the paper—she wasn't one of those tedious, meticulous unwrappers—and very carefully opened the box, checking out the contents before she shared it with everyone. It was…another box. She opened two more boxes until she got to the final box.

Sunny's mouth went dry. It was a jewelry box. She could deal with some nice earrings. She opened the hinged lid…except it wasn't earrings. A diamond ring sparkled against black satin.

Sunny's mind went blank. Blood rushed to her head.

"Marry me, Sunny," Cade said. "I've been waiting all my life for you." His tawny eyes were sincere but they held his ever-present wariness.

"Holy hell," Gracie blurted. Linc kicked her under the table.

The table erupted.

"'Bout damn time."

"Woohoo!"

"I told you she was a keeper."

"I knew from the beginning."

The ring was beautiful. He'd just proposed in front of the people that mattered most to him. But something didn't feel right.

"Why do you want to marry me?" she asked quietly but the whole table stopped talking abruptly as if she'd shouted it at him.

Cade gave her a what're-you-talking-about look. "It's not just because the sex is great."

Across the table from her, Georgia made a choking noise.

"It is great sex," Sunny acknowledged to Georgia. “I don’t imagine your man’s a slacker in that department, either. I think it’s probably a family trait.” Linc and Martin smirked. Cade scowled. She addressed herself to him. “But no, great sex is no reason to get married.”

“I just said that.”

“I was agreeing.”

He crossed his arms over his chest. “I’m sure we’ll have our ups and downs, but I think we’ll be happy together. We’re compatible.”

Compatible? He was grinding her heart beneath his heel. “Do you love me?”

“Dammit, Sunny, you know I’m not good at pretty speeches. You’re smart, strong, beautiful. I care about you.”

They’d iron this out right now. If she didn’t take a stand, she’d be lost forever. “I’m not asking for a pretty speech. I’m asking for a simple yes or no answer. Do you love me?”

He scowled at her. “Nothing has ever been simple with you. Neither is this. It’s complicated.”

She clutched the ring box in her hand. It was as complicated and as simple as what was in her heart. “I love you. I think I was in love with you before I ever met you and since then I’ve grown to love you more. We can argue and then kiss and make up. We can work through problems. That’s what couples do. That's what mates do. But none of it will work if you can't tell me you love me." She took a deep breath and stared him down, challenged him. "Do you love me, Cade Stone?"

Everyone held their breath. Even the house seemed to be waiting on his answer.

He gave her that hard, implacable stare she knew so well. The same unyielding expression he wore on the billboard. "No."

One syllable. Pain seared her, sliced her heart to ribbons.

"That was the wrong answer," Martin drawled.

"Oh, shit."

"Holy hell."

Sunny rubbed her thumb against her hummingbird ring and a calm flowed through her. "I can't heal you. You're the only one that can do that. And until you can tell me you love me, this doesn't mean anything." She placed the ring box on the table, laid her napkin beside her plate, and stood. "Until then, we don't have anything else to say to one another."

CADE WANTED TO HOWL as the door closed behind Sunny and she walked to her car, got in and drove away. What the hell was wrong with her? Why did she demand the one thing he couldn't give when he'd offered her everything else? His family sat frozen like statues.

"That was the most asinine thing I've ever seen you do, son," Martin drawled into the heavy silence.

"What did you just say?"

Martin stood and pushed his sleeves up. "I said I'm about to knock some sense into you. You've wanted this for a long time, so let's do it."

Martin was the one without any sense. Frustration boiled inside Cade. If Martin wanted a fight, he'd give him a fight. He shoved back from the table and pushed to his feet. "We'll take this outside. It won't be as far for you to get to your car afterward."

Cade stalked toward the back door and Martin mockingly bowed for Cade to go before him. Everyone rushed along behind them.

Cade and Martin faced off beneath the bare branches of a sprawling oak.

Gracie grabbed Linc's arm. "Stop them! Cade's going to kill Daddy."

"Don't be too sure," Linc said.

What the hell? Cade turned and glared at Linc.

Bam. Gracie screamed as the coppery taste of blood filled Cade's mouth and his ears rang. Son of a bitch! Martin had hit him while he was looking the other way.

Martin rubbed his knuckles and smirked. "I shoulda done that a long time ago."

Cade saw red. Instinctively he took a flying leap and knocked Martin to the ground, landing on top of him. He reared back to drive his fist into Martin's face…and stopped. Martin just lay there, making no move to protect himself.

"Go ahead," his father said, "hit me. If it'll make you feel better and it'll end this thing between us, hit me. Knock the everlivin' hell out of me if it'll make you feel better."

"Don't, Cade. Please," Gracie sobbed.

Martin didn't look away, his gaze boring into Cade. "Don't pay any attention to your sister. She doesn't understand. But I do understand, so go ahead and hit me."

Cade…couldn't. He rolled off of Martin and flopped onto his back in the winter-brown grass. "Get up," he said. "I can't hit you."

Martin sat up and waved his hand at everyone else. "Y'all go back in the house. The show's over out here."

Cade stayed on his back, staring up at the sky, bleakness eating at his soul. "Now what in the hell's your problem, boy? Anybody with a nugget of sense can see you're wall-eyed in love with that gal. Why'd you do a stupid thing and tell her you didn't love her? And in front of all of us? I'm not much for pretty speeches myself, but damn, even I know better than that."

"Love makes you weak."

"Where'd you ever get such a goddamn stupid notion?"

"You."

"Me?"

"I saw what happened when Mama died. I used to think you were damn near invincible and then…"

"You think it was loving her that made me weak?" Martin rubbed his hand over his face as if his very soul was weary. "You got it all wrong. Loving her made me a stronger man. What you saw afterward, that was *my* weakness. That was *me* learning to find my own strength without Lucy. It took me a while. I'm not as strong a man as you are, Cade. Those first couple of weeks, all I wanted to do was die. Those were dark days when all I wanted was the numbness found at the bottom of a bottle. I'm not proud that I wasn't there for you kids. Maybe you can't ever forgive me for that. I still think you'd feel better if you'd just hit me. But you've got to figure out that it's love that gives you your strength. It was your love for your brother and your sister that made you strong enough to do what you had to do. I'm not one of those touchy feely pansy-asses but I figured you kids always knew I loved you. That was the strength I found to put down the bottle. If I hadn't loved you kids and known you kids loved me, hell, I'd have just gone ahead and died. Weakness is being afraid to face down what scares the shit of you. It's a weak man or woman who turns away from love."

"Then what the hell was the whole four-week dating thing?"

"I told you I was bad at this talking business. Love only makes you stronger if you give it back. There's no strength in being a taker. There hadn't been anything in me to give to another woman since your mama died. Until now. Me and Marlene…we're gonna give it a go."

"Give it a go?"

"Yeah. Give it a go—married. I'm ribs and a beer and she's sushi with sake, which is some nasty stuff, let me tell you, son, but I love her and she seems to love me."

Martin stood and dusted off his britches. "Now get up and go make things right with your woman." He held out his hand to help Cade up.

Cade almost ignored it. Ten minutes ago he would've got to his feet on his own. He took his father's hand and let him pull him to his feet.

"We can talk anytime you want, son, but don't make me kick your ass again."

CADE STOOD ALONE beneath the tree. Suddenly all the hair on the back of his neck stood up. He looked over his shoulder. The wolf stood at the edge of the woods, watching him, seemingly waiting.

"Okay," he shouted, "I see you. I'm going now."

The wolf vanished behind a tree.

He got it. He didn't need to be hit over the head any longer. Obviously the wolf was trying to tell him something.

He slammed in the back door. Everyone stared at him as if he was off his rocker. Yeah, if he saw someone standing in the yard yelling at the woods, he'd think there was a little mental instability, too. Hell, maybe he *was* losing his mind.

"I'll be back," he said.

He marched down the hall to his desk in the den and sat down in front of his computer. Within a few minutes he'd found a suitable Web site. Sunny first. The hummingbird was a creature of joy. It was a reminder to those it encountered to look at the past and not wish for "what was" but rather extract the sweetness from the past and grab today's joy. To find the joy and sweetness of any situation, even if it meant delving deep beneath a bitter layer to find it. It fit her, like the pieces of an intricate puzzle falling into place.

He scrolled down to the wolf. Protector, loyalty to family, and fiercely loyal to a mate. He knew all of that. The next bit, however, held the message intended for him: finding inner strength and power was only achieved by facing one's deepest fear.

He sat back in his chair and closed his eyes. She'd known. Sunny knew him better than he knew himself. She was right, she couldn't do this for him. He would only be a whole man when he faced down his fear and allowed himself to love. And she deserved a whole man. In an instant of understanding, it all fell into place for him. What he had been too weak to grapple with on his own, he could now face for her, with her. Her love made him a stronger man, but only if he returned it. And he could only return it if he faced down his fear and gave her his heart.

He stood and walked back down the hall to the kitchen, feeling more at peace with himself than he had in a long, long time.

Conversation stopped when he walked in the room. "Come on, everyone. We're going to take a ride."

SUNNY PACED ACROSS HER LIVING ROOM, fuming. She should've whacked him upside his thick head. She knew he loved her. But the big Neanderthal had to own it. What was wrong with him?

She had a pretty good idea between his stupid four-week rule and what Gracie had divulged about their mother's death. She loved him but she wasn't going to be an enabler. What kind of woman would say yes to that proposal? The same woman who would agree to his stupid four-week rule, that's who. And that wasn't her.

All the ire went out of her, leaving her spent. She needed a plan. What kind of plan did someone make so that someone else would admit they loved them? God, that even sounded convoluted in her own head. It was like trying to figure out how to make the horse drink once you led it to water.

For about two seconds she considered accepting his ring, getting engaged but stipulating no wedding until she had an "I love you." Nope. Her gut response earlier had been right. She took a stand on this now or—

Someone pounded on her door and she nearly jumped out of her skin. She looked out the front window. Cade. And Georgia, Linc, Martin, Marlene, Gracie and Mark all congregated on the sidewalk behind him. She wasn't too sure whether they resembled a lynch mob or a support group.

Heart pounding, she opened the door and stepped outside. He stood on the third step down, putting them on eye level. "Yes?" Then she noticed the split in his lower lip and his swollen jaw. "What in the world happened to you?"

"He and Daddy got in a fight. Daddy hit him," Gracie piped up.

Oh, my God. They'd fought on Christmas Day. She almost reached out to touch him but caught herself. She pinned her arms to her side and hardened her heart. "I told you I didn't have anything else to say to you."

He shook his head. "That's not true. You said you didn't have anything else to say to me until I could tell you I love you. Okay. I do."

She wasn't sure if she understood what she thought he was saying. "You do what?"

"I do love you." He leaned back and yelled for the neighborhood at large, "I love Sunny Templeton."

His family cheered behind him. The neighbors to her right gave them all a suspicious look as they walked a visitor to their car.

She wanted to believe him, wanted to trust him, but…

He must have read her doubt because he continued. "I looked up the wolf. I got the message. I'll protect you, I'll walk with you but mostly I'll love you until I draw my last dying breath and then beyond that." No wariness shadowed his eyes.

Sunny felt as if she might burst with joy. She found herself at a loss for words. Instead, she trailed her finger over his swollen jaw.

Even with his jaw hurting and an audience behind them, desire flared in his eyes. "I think we should take this inside. You know I'm much better at showing than telling." He picked her up and tossed her over his shoulder.

"We're taking this private," he yelled over her to his family.

Laughing, she waved, upside-down, at her future in-laws. "Merry Christmas."

She had a feeling she was going to spend a lot of time looking at the world this way.

* * * * *

Turn the page for a sneak preview of the first book in the new miniseries
DIAMONDS DOWN UNDER
from Silhouette Desire®,
VOWS & A VENGEFUL GROOM
by Bronwyn Jameson

Available January 2008
(SD #1843)

Silhouette Desire®
Always Powerful, Passionate and Provocative

Kimberley Blackstone didn't notice the waiting horde of media until it was too late. Flashbulbs exploded around her like a New Year's light show. She skidded to a halt, so abruptly her trailing suitcase all but overtook her.

This had to be a case of mistaken identity. Surely. Kimberley hadn't been on the paparazzi hit list for close to a decade, not since she'd estranged herself from her billionaire father and his headline-hungry diamond business.

But no, it was *her* name they called. *Her* face was the focus of a swarm of lenses that circled her like avid hornets. Her heart started to pound with fear-fueled adrenaline.

What did they want?

What was going on?

With a rising sense of bewilderment she

scanned the crowd for a clue, and her gaze fastened on a tall, leonine figure forcing his way to the front. A tall, familiar figure. Her head came up in stunned recognition, and their gazes collided across the sea of heads before the cameras erupted with another barrage of flashes, this time right in her exposed face.

Blinded by the flashbulbs—and by the shock of that momentary eye-meet—Kimberley didn't realize his intent until he'd forged his way to her side, possibly by the sheer strength of his personality. She felt his arm wrap around her shoulder, pulling her into the protective shelter of his body, allowing her no time to object. No chance to lift her hands to ward him off.

In the space of a hastily drawn breath, she found herself plastered knee-to-nose against six feet two inches of hard-bodied male.

Ric Perrini.

Her lover for ten torrid weeks, her husband for ten tumultuous days.

Her ex for ten tranquil years.

After all this time, he should not have felt so familiar but, oh dear, he did. She knew the scent of that body and its lean, muscular strength. She knew its heat and its slick power and every response it could draw from hers.

She also recognized the ease with which he'd taken control of the moment and the decisiveness of his deep voice when it rumbled close to her ear. "I have a car waiting outside. Is this your only luggage?"

Kimberley nodded. "I assume you will tell me," she said tightly, "what this welcome party is all about."

"Not while the welcome party is within earshot. No."

Barking a request for the cameramen to stand aside, Perrini took her hand and pulled her into step with his ground-eating stride. Kimberley let him, because he was right, damn his arrogant, Italian-suited hide. Despite the speed with which he whisked her across the airport terminal, she could almost feel the hot breath of the pursuing media on her back.

This was neither the time nor the place for explanations. Inside his car, however, she would get answers.

Now that the initial shock had been blown away—by the haste of their retreat, by the heat of her gathering indignation, by the rush of adrenaline fired by Perrini's presence and the looming verbal battle—her brain was starting to tick over. This had to be her father's doing. And if it was a Howard Blackstone publicity ploy, then it had to be about Blackstone Diamonds, the company that ruled his life.

The knowledge made her chest tighten with a familiar ache of disillusionment.

She'd known her father would be flying in from Sydney for today's opening of the newest in his chain of exclusive, high-end jewelry boutiques. The opulent shop front sat adjacent to the rival business where Kimberley worked. No coincidence, she thought bitterly, just as it was no coincidence that Ric Perrini was here in Auckland ushering her to his car.

Perrini was Howard Blackstone's right-hand man, second in command at Blackstone Diamonds, a legacy of his short-lived marriage to the boss's daughter. No doubt her father had sent him to fetch her; the question was *why?*

* * * * *

Get swept away down under with the glitz and glamour of the Blackstone empire as Kimberley tries to determine the real reason behind her "reunion" with Ric....

Look for VOWS & A VENGEFUL GROOM
by Bronwyn Jameson
in stores January 2008.

When Kimberley Blackstone's father is presumed dead, Kimberley is required to take over the helm of Blackstone Diamonds. She has to work closely with her ex, Ric Perrini, to battle not only the press, but also the fierce attraction still sizzling between them. Does Ric feel the same...or is it the power her share of Blackstone Diamonds will provide him as he battles for boardroom supremacy.

Look for

VOWS &
A VENGEFUL GROOM

by

BRONWYN
JAMESON

Available January wherever you buy books

Visit Silhouette Books at www.eHarlequin.com SD76843

To fulfill his father's dying wish, Greek tycoon Christos Niarchos must marry Ava Monroe, a woman who betrayed him years ago. But his soon-to-be-wife has a secret that could rock more than his passion for her.

Look for

THE GREEK TYCOON'S SECRET HEIR

by

KATHERINE GARBERA

Available January wherever you buy books

Visit Silhouette Books at www.eHarlequin.com SD76845

REQUEST YOUR FREE BOOKS!

2 FREE NOVELS PLUS 2 FREE GIFTS!

Red-hot reads!

YES! Please send me 2 FREE Harlequin® Blaze® novels and my 2 FREE gifts. After receiving them, if I don't wish to receive any more books, I can return the shipping statement marked "cancel." If I don't cancel, I will receive 6 brand-new novels every month and be billed just $3.99 per book in the U.S., or $4.47 per book in Canada, plus 25¢ shipping and handling per book and applicable taxes, if any*. That's a savings of at least 15% off the cover price! I understand that accepting the 2 free books and gifts places me under no obligation to buy anything. I can always return a shipment and cancel at any time. Even if I never buy another book from Harlequin, the two free books and gifts are mine to keep forever.

151 HDN EF3W 351 HDN EF3X

Name (PLEASE PRINT)

Address Apt.

City State/Prov. Zip/Postal Code

Signature (if under 18, a parent or guardian must sign)

Mail to the **Harlequin Reader Service®:**
IN U.S.A.: P.O. Box 1867, Buffalo, NY 14240-1867
IN CANADA: P.O. Box 609, Fort Erie, Ontario L2A 5X3

Not valid to current Harlequin Blaze subscribers.

Want to try two free books from another line?
Call 1-800-873-8635 or visit www.morefreebooks.com.

* Terms and prices subject to change without notice. NY residents add applicable sales tax. Canadian residents will be charged applicable provincial taxes and GST. This offer is limited to one order per household. All orders subject to approval. Credit or debit balances in a customer's account(s) may be offset by any other outstanding balance owed by or to the customer. Please allow 4 to 6 weeks for delivery.

Your Privacy: Harlequin is committed to protecting your privacy. Our Privacy Policy is available online at www.eHarlequin.com or upon request from the Reader Service. From time to time we make our lists of customers available to reputable firms who may have a product or service of interest to you. If you would prefer we not share your name and address, please check here. ☐

HB07

Inside ROMANCE

Stay up-to-date on all your
romance reading news!

Inside Romance is a FREE quarterly newsletter
highlighting our upcoming series releases
and promotions.

Visit

www.eHarlequin.com/InsideRomance

to sign up to receive our complimentary newsletter today!

IRN1107

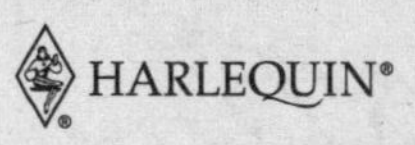

INTRIGUE®

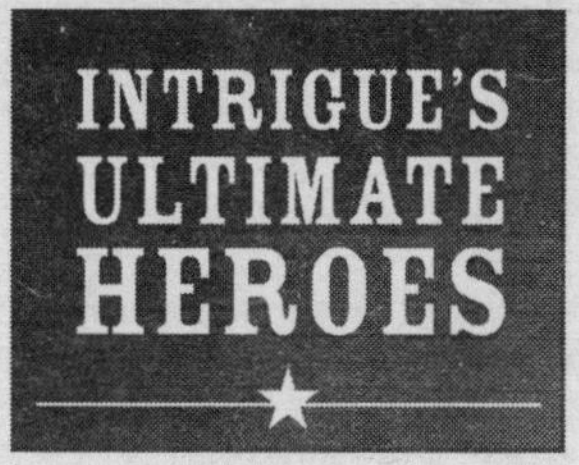

6 heroes. 6 stories.
One month to read them all.

For one special month, Harlequin Intrigue is dedicated to those heroes among men. Desirable doctors, sexy soldiers, brave bodyguards—they are all Intrigue's Ultimate Heroes.

In January, collect all 6.

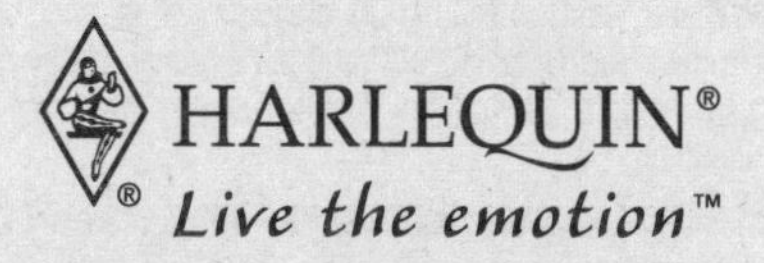

www.eHarlequin.com

HI69302

COMING NEXT MONTH

#369 ONE WILD WEDDING NIGHT Leslie Kelly
Blaze Encounters—One blazing book, five sizzling stories
Girls just want to have fun.... And for five bridesmaids, their friend's wedding night is the perfect time for the rest of them to let loose. After all, love is in the air. And so, they soon discover, is great sex...

#370 MY GUILTY PLEASURE Jamie Denton
The Martini Dares, Bk. 3
The trial is supposed to come first for the legal-eagle duo of Josephine Winfield and Sebastian Stanhope. But the long hours—and sizzling attraction—are taking their toll. Is it a simple case of lust in the first degree? Or dare she think there's more?

#371 BARE NECESSITIES Marie Donovan
A sexy striptease ignites an intense affair between longtime friends Adam Hale, a play-by-the-rules financial trader, and Bridget Weiss, a break-all-the-rules lingerie designer. But what will happen to their friendship now that their secret lust for each other is no longer a secret?

#372 DOES SHE DARE? Tawny Weber
Blush
When no-nonsense Isabel Santos decides to make a "man plan," she never dreams she'll have a chance to try it out with the guy who inspired it—her high school crush, hottie Dante Luciano. He's still everything she's ever wanted. And she'll make sure she's everything he'll *never* forget....

#373 AT YOUR COMMAND Julie Miller
Marry in haste? Eighteen months ago Captain Zachariah Clark loved, married, then left Becky Clark. Now Zach's back home, and he's suddenly realized he knows nothing about his wife except her erogenous zones. Then again, great sex isn't such a bad place to start....

#374 THE TAO OF SEX Jade Lee
Extreme
Landlord Tracy Williams wants to sell her building, almost as much as she wants her tenant, sexy Nathan Gao. But when Nathan puts a sale at risk by giving Tantric classes, Tracy has to bring a stop to them. That is, until he offers her some private *hands-on* instruction...

www.eHarlequin.com

HBCNM1207